PENGUIN BOOKS

THE TESTIMONY OF TALIESIN JONES

Rhidian Brook originally comes from Tenby, South Wales. He now lives in London with his wife Nicola and his son Gabriel. In addition to his highly acclaimed first novel, *The Testimony of Taliesin Jones*, he is the author of *Jesus and the Adman*. Rhidian divides his time between advertising and work on his third novel.

RHIDIAN BROOK

The Testimony of Taliesin Jones

PENGUIN BOOKS

PENGUIN BOOKS

Published by the Penguin Group
Penguin Putnam Inc., 375 Hudson Street,
New York, New York 10014, U.S.A.
Penguin Books Ltd, 80 Strand, London WC2R 0RL, England
Penguin Books Australia Ltd, 250 Camberwell Road,
Camberwell, Victoria 3124, Australia
Penguin Books Canada Ltd, 10 Alcorn Avenue,
Toronto, Ontario, Canada M4V 3B2
Penguin Books India (P) Ltd, 11 Community Centre,
Panchsheel Park, New Delhi – 110 017, India
Penguin Books (N.Z.) Ltd, Cnr Rosedale and Airborne Roads,
Albany, Auckland, New Zealand
Penguin Books (South Africa) (Pty) Ltd, 24 Sturdee Avenue,
Rosebank, Johannesburg 2196, South Africa

Penguin Books Ltd, Registered Offices:
Harmondsworth, Middlesex, England

First published in Great Britain by Flamingo,
an imprint of HarperCollinsPublishers, 1996
First published in the United States of America by Penguin Books 2002

1 3 5 7 9 10 8 6 4 2

PUBLISHER'S NOTE
This is a work of fiction. Names, characters, places, and incidents either
are the product of the author's imagination or are used fictitiously, and any
resemblance to actual persons, living or dead, business establishments,
events, or locales is entirely coincidental.

CIP data available
ISBN 0 14 20.0157 0

Printed in the United States of America
Set in Bembo

For my mothers and fathers,
brothers and sisters

AUTHOR'S NOTE

It may help the reader to note that the correct pronunciation of the main character's name, Taliesin, is Taly-essin.

CHAPTER ONE

❧

His latest book is an atlas: *The Atlas of the World*. Its jacket depicts a bright blue spherical earth turning against a dark red background. He takes the protective jacket off and sees that the title of the book is embossed in gold lettering against a darker blood-red background. There is no earth on the hard cover. He strokes the cool surface of this expensive book and leaves a slight handprint – his hands hot with anticipation. Then he runs his index finger along the grooves of the gold lettering and feels the indentations: up and down the v's of the W; round and round the O of WORLD.

He opens the book and releases a smell of paper, a fresh smell that reminds him of exercise books distributed at the beginning of a new school year: green for Geography, pink for Biology, grey for Religious Education. On the clear white page is a handwritten message. It reads: 'Darling Taliesin, wishing you a very happy eleventh birthday, love Mum xxx'.

His mother's writing is the sensible, flowing cursive of a Grown-Up; all her letters join without evidence of a break. It will be four or maybe five years before he can string his letters together like that. His mother's writing is the acme of handwriting; it has a perfect lean, a consistent spacing and it is legible without being bland.

After the message she's put three crosses, each with a value of one kiss. This is restrained for her. It represents a distinct decline in affection. Her letters are usually sprinkled with kisses that overspill to the outside of the envelope. Perhaps she was sobered by the seriousness and expensiveness of the book; she didn't want to demean its science by covering it in too many kisses. Or perhaps these three kisses represent her new family unit: Mr Rapunzel, Leo the cat and herself.

He picks up the solid, satisfying book and smells it again, hoping that some molecules of perfume drifted from his mother's wrist as she wrote and that he might now detect a whiff of her. But the book just exudes an overwhelming odour of newness; a distant coolness.

It came the day before his birthday, hand-delivered by the postman, in a promising brown envelope tied with string in a cross, and bearing the tantalizing instruction 'Do not open until September 14th.' He also received a rust-coloured, one hundred per cent Shetland Wool jumper fortified and water-proofed with lanolin to protect him from Welsh Rain. His mother always gives him fawn-coloured clothes because fawn colours are his colours, apparently. He was pleased with the book.

He turns the white, white pages which are so thick they give the impression of being more than one page stuck together. He travels through the title pages: past the Fore-word, the Contents, a list of the countries and cities of the world, a section on stars with their alien names and patterns, a section on the universe which begins with the words 'We do not yet know how the universe came about.' He travels on through a section on the more local solar system and the planets that he knows in order from Mercury to Pluto.

Then comes The Earth in cross-sectional globes with God-sized bites taken out of them to reveal crusts, mantles and cores. The outer core and the red-hot inner core remind him of a peach.

A geological timescale spirals up the page and shows man arriving late, making his mark in the last fraction of the green coloured Tertiary period. He follows the names back through time: Cretaceous, Jurassic, on backwards past

Devonian as far back as the inner swirl of the spiral which whirls through Cambrian and Pre-Cambrian and ends in a period called Archaean and speculative dates with question marks. Even this all-knowing, comprehensive book doesn't have all the answers. There are no real explanations as to how the earth was made and what set it spinning on its axis, tilted at an angle of such vital precision.

A shaggy man with a spear stands at the top of the next chart leading a procession of animals that recede back through time: a monkey, a stunted horse, a blue whale, some shells, and then dinosaurs which cover a large section of the chart before legs become tails and flippers, and reptiles become fish. These in turn become shells and seaweed. After this there are blank years and question marks again.

On into the book. Continents splitting, volcanoes spitting, temperatures dropping and then rising. Different coloured maps of the world divided into many categories: minerals, vegetation, energy, food production. There are apples in Japan, apparently. And then the normal maps; the maps that just show where everything is.

The first map is of the world and it shows countries divided into pastel yellow, pink, orange, green and lilac and the sea a light blue. The world is an amazing series of shapes without symmetry. A massive Africa fills the middle of the spread, too close to the sun and too big; India points an exotic nose into a warm-sounding sea; North America bends like a tree in a fast-moving wind. No two places look the same.

He turns the page and moves closer to home – to Europe with its fine outlines and many borders. Where the pages meet in the centre a tiny pink Britain and an even tinier indistinct Wales are lost in the crease of the book. On the next page Britain appears big enough to show the beast-head shape of his home country. Is it a pig? Is it an ugly man? Is it a dragon? Every country has a shape. School teachers have told him that. Italy is a boot kicking a Sicilian football. His

3

geography teacher described Wales as a boar's head but he sees it as a dragon, which, when he half closes his eyes, has a snout that shoots fire.

He looks for the names he knows, for his own village and for the town where his mother now lives. His village is there somewhere, unmarked amongst the browns and the darkish relief greens. His mother's town is big enough to be indicated (he sees it there, snuggling into the mouth of the dragon). But his own village isn't shown. He gauges where it should be and measures the distance between it and his mother's town as being a thumb and a half. In reality this is a distance of some fifty miles.

There is no larger scale map of Wales in the atlas, so to compensate for this he continues to increase the scale for himself, in his head. He moves his head slowly towards the page closing up like a camera, and then he continues the journey in his head, flying on and down. And as he magnifies the scale the distance between himself and his mother increases.

CHAPTER TWO

❧

THROUGH THE still-growing eyes of Taliesin Jones, the morning village looks as if it will never wake from a particularly long summer. This year summer is oversleeping into autumn and The Man On The Telly talks about Indian Summer. Taliesin pictures Welsh Summer visiting India on a meteorological exchange and Indians walking around Bombay saying, 'Ah, look, it is a Welsh Summer – what bad luck.'

There is a silver glint on the road. Cwmglum's ugly houses blink at the low-angled sun which refracts through milk bottles onto mats. Some people have poked notes into the bottles to specify the number of pints they want, confident that there won't be rain to wash away their requests. A cat rubs against the empties, time on its paws.

Taliesin knows that the houses are ugly because he has seen *Villages of Britain* – a book in his father's bedroom. In that book the sun is always shining and the sky is a postcard blue. The houses are a too-good-to-be-true pretty, like houses that Hansel and Gretel might have lived in; black and white cottages that bend under the weight of oldness.

Cwmglum's houses are not that old and they do not feature in *Villages of Britain*. To those who live here the village is neither beautiful nor ugly; exciting nor boring. How could they know when most of them have never read *Villages of Britain*? Ignorance has made the heart grow indifferent. Even Taliesin (who isn't ignorant because he's seen the book) thinks the village doesn't look too bad when the sun is

5

out like it is today. Its untimely rays forgive the ugliness, soften the colours and give everything a potential.

This morning Taliesin feels this potential like a bubble at the back of his head, lifting him up, willing him to see more of what is around him. This feeling is commissioning him to be a bard and to eulogise this village of his which has a name that sounds like the noise water makes in boots; its slate-roof houses, its pub, its double-Welsh bus timetable, its opulent greengrocer and its chapel, stubborn as a goat on the hill. It almost doesn't matter that his village isn't marked in his atlas, or that it doesn't feature in *Villages of Britain*. This is his world. This is where he was put. He isn't a goatherd in Afghanistan or a banana separator in Brazil. He is him here, not them there, and it feels planned that way.

Right now he feels his own significance more acutely than ever before. Almost as if the world has all been created for his benefit and that he is the only one who is aware of its existence. Everyone else is here for decoration. This moment now, the sun, the village, the way the sun falls on the village, the lateness of summer, the soft calm of the day – they are all for him. He could be the only person truly alive in the world.

Taliesin walks past the bus stop and swings a 360° on it. The bus stop is a post with an indistinguishable and unfathomable both-ways timetable in English and Welsh. Whatever the timetable may say there is always time before the bus comes. And this is his favourite time.

Across the road, pushing a broom along the pavement, the greengrocer's wife sweeps the shop front. Taliesin can see her blue-rinse hair clearly this morning. Last week it was a confused white-grey, today it is a livid purple. It is also curly and short, the way old women's hair is. He never sees an old woman with long hair. It's always cut short or in a bun – and blue.

Handycott, the grocer, is arranging his fruit, talking to them and petting them as if they were his children. The sun

6

bathes his display in an edible light. All the fare is laid out with an artist's eye for colour and composition: the green apples contrasting with the red; the caulies and cabbages offsetting the broccoli; the potatoes lined up in ascending order of size; tomatoes, oranges and apples forming traffic light rows. The apples are prominent in the canvas. They are the grocer's pride and joy; his choicest fruit. He is emptying a fresh box of them now, fussing and cosseting them as he would a youngest daughter. He says that his love for his fruit makes them taste better and Taliesin believes him.

The grocer is a big man, his frame comfortably carrying a middle-aged corpulence. His eyes have heavy bags, as does his chin. He has no hair on his head but plenty on his face. Taliesin calls him Walrus (never to his face), because of his massive build and delicate curling moustache. He has no children of his own. He can't have them. According to Jonathan, Taliesin's brother, Walrus had his balls raked in a game of rugby and that was it for him.

Taliesin crosses the road.

The grocer is humming and emptying apples into one of the display trays. He too is bathed in sunlight and Taliesin has to squint as he follows the big man's movements. Taliesin is always his first customer of the day.

'Good morning,' the grocer says.

'Hello,' Taliesin replies.

'And how are you this beautiful Tuesday morning?'

'I'm tidy,' Taliesin says. He looks and wonders at the polished fruit. He tries to think of all the countries they come from: bananas from Brazil, oranges from Spain, pears from England.

'Good birthday?'

'Yes. Thank you.'

'So, how does it feel to be eleven?' the grocer asks, now turning the apples stalk-up in the tray.

'I don't feel that different, really,' Taliesin says.

7

'Did you get what you wanted?'

'Books.' Taliesin nods to show that this is what he wanted.

The grocer's wife, a frightening woman, walks to the front of the shop and takes the broom back inside. 'Morning,' she says, in a voice that is deep for a woman.

'Morning,' Taliesin says. No soubriquets for her, not even in his head. He cannot understand how a man as genial as the grocer could be married to a woman so fierce. The grocer is as fearful of her as Taliesin is; he has to check that she is out of ear and eye shot before conversing. The door closes and Walrus turns and places a hand on Taliesin's head, measuring him.

'You're not exactly a bean are you? You're more of a potato – you grow at a steady pace. Anyway, there's no hurry. Make the most of being young, that's what I say.'

Taliesin has never considered being anything else. The here and now is what matters to him, not tomorrow, nor even yesterday. It's only those around him who show concern for their age and the passing of time: his brother with his attempts at shaving, his mother with her inappropriately youthful haircuts, his father with his plans for an impossible future.

'The trick is to give up childish ways and still see things like a child: simply and clearly, without the clutter of opinion. You mustn't be in a hurry to be grown-up.' The man looks down wistfully at the boy, remembering his own quick ripe youth. He then bends over and pulls off some unripened bananas, still green.

'Here, look.' He snaps one from the bunch. 'Nearly ready but not quite. If you ate him now he'd taste terrible – sour and hard and he'd give you indigestion. But give him some more of this sun and he'll soon taste sweet. It doesn't take long. Can't force it, see. Things need time to perfect. You can't trick time.'

'It's only other people who tell me to grow up,' Taliesin

8

points out. He thinks of his brother trying to be older than he is, wanting desperately to be a man. His balls have dropped, he constantly asserts his age advantage and athleticism. He shaves, even though the fluffy down isn't bristle yet and he daily reminds his younger brother that being a child is a pathetic state that we have to suffer before gaining the freedoms of adult life. Taliesin thinks about the grocer's crushed balls and his own balls waiting for the signal, the inevitable drop to manhood. No way of stopping it. Nothing he can do about it except wish for the Never Never dropping balls of Peter Pan.

'I liked being seven. Things were easier when I was seven. No one told me to grow up then, they just let me be seven,' he says.

The grocer laughs at this.

'There you are! You're talking like a real grown-up already, remembering the good old days when you were seven, when life was easier. That's when you know you're a grown-up, when you start to look back.'

Taliesin sneezes.

'You could do with some vitamin C.'

'What's got the most vitamin C?' Taliesin asks, assessing the various candidates.

The grocer doesn't hesitate in taking an oval hairy fruit the size of an egg from a small box behind the bananas. He holds it in front of Taliesin's nose. Taliesin takes it and is repulsed by the texture of it.

'These are new. Don't even have them in West Haven. Kiwi fruit, from New Zealand. It's what keeps the All Blacks so fit. They're never sick because they eat these all the time.' Taliesin pictures the All Blacks but he can't imagine them eating ugly egg shaped fruit. He sees them doing their dance, the Haka. They're slapping their knees and waving their hands and making faces like cannibals and chanting, 'Takani, takani, kanawi, hoopla, hoopla.' It's impossible to imagine

9

them eating this peculiar little fruit with skin like an old man's. Not everything the grocer says is true.

'Feels funny. How do you eat it?' he asks.

'Some prefer to eat it with a spoon, like a boiled egg. But I like to eat it with the skin on, just like an apple.'

'I'd prefer an apple,' Taliesin says, handing back the kiwi.

'Which one is it to be then?' the grocer asks again.

Taliesin looks at the different apples on display, at the tempting American Reds whose flesh is always sleepy. This is the fairy tale apple; the apple that the Wicked Queen offered Snow White and that William Tell balanced on his son's head. Next to these are some Golden Russets. The grocer says that the Golden Russet is an interesting apple, with a crisp and delicate taste. Then there is Taliesin's own favourite: the yellow Golden Delicious, which the grocer insists is a bland apple with a misleading name. 'It's all juice and no flavour,' he says. And at the end of the row, the red and green Cox's Pippin, with the leaves still on the stalks.

'Golden Delicious, please,' Taliesin says.

The grocer is disappointed at this choice.

'The young always seem to prefer it. But I think it's about time you tried the king of apples. So much better than that bland Delicious. In fact, I insist that you do.' The grocer leans over the appropriate carton and selects a Cox's Pippin. 'Here. Sshh. This one's free. Don't let my Missus see. This one's good enough for Eve. "Have an apple, go to chapel," as they say.'

Taliesin weighs the apple in his hand. With its leaf it looks the archetypal apple. Indeed, it could be the apple that Eve picked. He remembers the picture in his *Illustrated Bible*, the one where Eve, despite God's prohibition, has taken the apple and a vast hand bursts through cloud to admonish her. That hand and Eve's nakedness are the things that stuck in his mind. Jonathan told him that the story of Adam and Eve wasn't true because there were dinosaurs before men. 'That's fuckin' rubbish,' he'd said. But Jonathan thought everything was fuckin' rubbish these days. When Taliesin asked his usually talkative father he received only shrugs and from his mother a sympathetic pat for asking such a lovely question. Then Mr Tower, his RE teacher, said that the story was not to be taken literally. Apparently it was a creation story; a myth with truths, he said. Maybe Walrus will know for sure if it's true or not – he knows about apples.

'Is that story about Adam and Eve true?' Taliesin asks.

The Walrus doesn't flinch as others have done.

'Yes, most certainly,' he says. 'It might not be accurate fact, like. It's just a way of showing something; a way of explaining how man fell out with God. It shows how men and women have a choice to listen to God or ignore Him.'

The grocer takes the apple back from Taliesin and holds it up close spotting a blemish. He rubs it on his apron and looks again. Deciding that it isn't clean enough, he takes another one from the box and does the same thing.

'Would it have been a Cox's that she picked?' Taliesin asks.

'Well, it would have to have been an apple that was too good to say no to; an apple that looked as good as it tasted. Most definitely a Cox's. Had to be. The Red is too obvious. The Russet is too small. Perhaps if it had been a Golden Delicious she wouldn't have bothered picking it and we might still be in Eden. Imagine that.' The grocer enjoys this speculation and chuckles to himself. Taliesin tries to imagine it. There are no maps of Eden in his *Atlas of the World*. He looked for it in the Middle Eastern section – that was where he was told it might be. He couldn't see it anywhere. His father told him that it might have had a different name then. Mesopotamia or something.

The grocer now holds an orange.

'Now an orange wouldn't have worked. Too messy and the wrong height. An orange would have been too much of a disincentive – all that peeling and juice squirting in her eye.

No. It had to be an apple. Here. This is a better one.' The grocer hands him an apple clean enough to be the first fruit plucked by man or woman. Holding it in his hand, Taliesin can see why Eve would have picked it. Impossible to resist. He would have done the same thing himself. Falling out with God was as simple as that. As he pictures it he sees his own mother as Eve reaching for the fruit.

'Of course, some say that it was a pomegranate that she picked,' the grocer says. 'Now there is a complicated fruit. But I'll go with the apple. It fits. Here take it before she sees,' the grocer says, as his wife scuttles through the back of the shop. Taliesin spirits the apple away into his satchel just as she appears at the back, her head moving above the shelves like a shark's dorsal fin.

'Enjoy it,' the grocer whispers.

The bizarre sun is rising, still tricking the village that it's summer. Taliesin feels a thrilling certainty, although he's not sure what he's certain about. This talk of Eden and Eve fires him. He still has that sense of heightened potential like a lovely pressure in his head, lifting him up, helping him to see more in what is around him. He feels like Adam, before the apple was picked, when he saw things clearly and felt secure that everything had been created for him. In those pre-apple days, Adam could hear God walking through the garden in the cool and occasionally God would push His hand through a cloud to let him know He was there. There was no dispute with God then. There were no choices to make. That apple changed everything.

CHAPTER THREE

❧

THE LIGHT SHINES through the classroom skylight in a
straight column, highlighting dust and other usually unseen
dead matter. Part of the light falls on Taliesin's face, causing
him to close his eyes and receive its heat. There are other
children moving around the room, taking time to settle
down. Some days get on with it, they pass anonymously
without drawing attention to themselves. Yet today has a
slow resonance, a heightened sense of significance which
Taliesin cannot really place.

Taliesin is a small boy for his age, although his feet are big
for his size. This gives his mother hope that he will turn out a
reasonable height in the end. 'Big feet; big man,' she always
says. His lack of height bothers others more than it does him.
People are always trying to compensate for his small stature
with tall observations about his latest growth spurt. If all
these remarks were true he'd be bursting through clouds by
now. When others tell him how much he's grown, he doesn't
disagree; he knows they mean well and that they're lying.
Today the grocer was closer to the truth without being
insulting. If he is growing he isn't seeing it. It's happening
imperceptibly and at a different rate from the saplings and
buds around him. In this pre-adolescent wood he is a bonsai
amongst bamboo.

His limbs are at least in proportion and his features are fine.
People say he has his father's eyes and his mother's hair and
nose, but he prefers to think of them as his own. His eyes are
wide and tear shaped. His hair is thick and straight and ruffled

frequently by the tall and the old. His skin is fair enough to freckle but dark enough to turn a light copper in an Indian Summer. A chipped front incisor has made him self-conscious about smiling and nervous of overzealous playground games. It is partly for this reason that he has an unfair reputation for being a loner at school, where he is only reasonably popular and known as 'Worm'.

'Worm' is a term of endearment or derogation depending on who says it and how they say it. His enemies call him 'Worm' to remind him of his diminutive build; his friends call him 'Worm' in reference to his love of books and incessant reading of them. He is a copious reader, burying himself in stories, burrowing deep into their other worlds and losing himself there. This a source of great irritation to his teachers. The glass-fronted cabinet in the corner of the form room already contains the first confiscation of the year – *Animal Farm*, impounded by his form teacher, Mr Davies. Mr Davies has promised to return it in time for the holiday, 'When there will be plenty of time for reading.' But ten weeks is too long to wait and see what happens to that horse, Boxer, so he has borrowed another copy of the book and this sits in the side pocket of his satchel, ready for the journey home.

There is a third meaning in his nickname, although few have appreciated it. Like a worm, Taliesin likes to get into the core of things – through a slow and persistent questioning. Questions are sweet apples to be eaten and this worm has a taste for all kinds. He questioned from an early age, maybe as early as two or three, pointing at an object and saying, 'Called? What called?' His parents were always happy to humour this hunger and provide the appropriate name: piano, potato, perfume. It seemed they had a word for everything he could point at. Then he discovered books with pictures and labels and names for all kinds of things, and for a time they provided all the answers. Then, quite suddenly, and without being asked, he found himself in rooms with other children listening to Grown-Ups who asked him questions. He was good at giving answers but he found it less rewarding than asking questions. His teachers noticed this and commented, 'If you spent more time listening you might not have to ask so many questions,' or 'Too many questions, not enough answers, boy.' Like Mr Kipling's 'Elephant Child' (a story for which he has developed a deep affinity) he was looking to get his nose bitten. He too, it seemed, suffered from insatiable curiosity.

Taliesin wasn't entirely happy with the role reversal that school imposed. It didn't seem fair that Grown-Ups, who theoretically had answers in the truck load, were now asking him for answers. He needed to ask more questions still, not because he wanted to distract, avoid or gain attention, but simply because there were so many questions to be asked – thousands of them in fact, all queuing up, knocking on the door of his mind, demanding answers. It didn't matter whether they were answered by book, teacher or father, for just as soon as the curling head of a question was cut off another appeared in its place, like some overcurious Hydra.

Oddly his parents, his teachers, even his books, didn't have the answers to all of his questions. They always tried to give him one, rather than admit that they didn't know; or worse, they would tell him to stop asking too many questions. They kept trying, O Dearly Beloved, to send him down to the dark, grey, greasy banks of the Limpopo River in the hope that he would get his nose bitten.

At the age of seven he had his first meeting with adult fallibility. His grandfather, a bald man with a leathery skin who smelt of cigars and old car seats, was giving him a general knowledge test, asking the names of rivers, mountains and capital cities. When he asked him what the capital of America was, Taliesin became confused, his head filling with images of skyscrapers. He knew he was wrong but rather than not give the answer he said, 'New York.' His grandfather then patted him on the back and started to congratulate him. Taliesin felt uncomfortable with the praise.

'Is that right, Grandpa?' he asked, perturbed.

'Yes, yes, of course, New York,' his grandfather assured him.

Later that night Taliesin checked his globe. New York was there, in bold letters signifying importance; and Washington was there, also in bold, but underlined to signify a capital city.

Before long he had succeeded in getting a number of Grown-Ups, including his mother and father, to say 'I don't know' to a number of testing queries. His questions moved on from the one-word-answer-fact-type questions that had answers in textbooks, to more abstract and subjective problems; to questions that genuinely seemed to have no one, singular, incontestable answer. Even teachers were found wanting.

If there are questions at the moment they are minor ones. How long will summer last? Are warts infectious?

As the form teacher enters the classroom Taliesin remains seated, tilting his head into the warm light pouring through the ceiling window. On his finger his has noticed a change in the smoothness of his skin and the appearance of an opaque hardening lump. While Mr Davies calls the register Taliesin places his finger into the stream of light and hopes for the beams to burn the wart away.

Mr Davies is having difficulty with the simple task of taking registration. There is a superlative stupidity about the class today. This weather is distracting. No one wants to be here. The teacher's voice is lost in a chorus of menagerie noises that only children and animals seem able to make. The surnames recite themselves until Taliesin's own approaches.

'Jones, Taliesin?'

'Sir.'

'Jones, William?'

'Here Sir.'

'Lewis?'

'Sir.'

'Morgan? . . . Morgan? Where's Morgan?'

'He's dead, Sir.'

'He's sunbathing, Sir.'

'All right, all right. Pugh?'

'Yup.'

'Yup? What is "Yup"? You're not a dog.'

'Woof . . . woof'

'Yup . . . yup'

'Ruff . . . ruff'

'All right, that's enough. Pugh!'

'Yes Sir, sorry Sir.'

'Rolley?'

'I'm right here, Sir.'

'Just answer the question, Rolley.'

'I did, Sir.'

'Tanner?'

'Mr Davies, please, Sir, can you tell Hooper to stop flicking my ears?'

'You're dead,' Hooper says.

'Right, quiet everyone. Quiet! Please.'

Despite these protestations the noise continues to bubble. Mr Davies is too nice, he strikes no fear. Everyone has a soft spot for his chubby face, fat lips and thick bufflehead of hair that sits in the middle of his head like a brown cloud. He is like a batty uncle who was born to be ridiculed and loved.

Hooper belts Tanner over the back of his head.

'Hooper! Here.' Mr Davies grimaces at the sound of his own shouting. He isn't built for shouting. Hooper moves casually to the front, clinging to his class-tough status, defiant like that Spartacus. He partially conceals a compass in his hand. Taliesin marvels at Hooper's confidence; nothing seems to scare him.

'I am getting tired of punishing you, Hooper. It seems that you never learn. Punishing you is punishing me. I just don't know if there's any point in punishing you anymore. What am I going to do with you?'

'I never did nothing.' Hooper doesn't even bother with a 'Sir'.

'You never did nothing?'

'Never!'

'Hooper, please, I'm not blind. I saw you hit Tanner. You hit him a minute ago.'

'I never.'

Hooper has deliberately failed to do his tie up and his trousers are definitely not regulation grey. How long can he keep up like this? The trouble is he'll use up his rebelliousness too early and end up being normal when he's a Grown-Up. He'll probably work in a bank at Prescelli.

Mr Davies looks imploringly at the class. No one dares implicate Hoop The Mental.

'I don't want to give you more lines, Hooper. You can do something useful, something constructive.' Mr Davies turns to the class again. 'What punishment shall I give Hooper?'

No one says a thing.

'Come on. You decide, I'm fed up with dishing out punishments, you decide.'

There are a few furtive giggles. It's a good idea, but there are risks, there are consequences, future retribution.

'Give 'm lunch duty, Sir,' Tanner says, still sore. 'Or he could clean the graffiti.'

The class are silently thinking of worse. There's torture, there's burning at the stake, there's firing squad. Tanner would really like Hooper to be strapped in a chair and have his ears flicked by the whole school. If only they could be sure that Hooper wouldn't survive. Of course, he'd come back like those irrepressible killers that never die in films. Hooper looks on with his arms folded, daring anyone to suggest anything more.

Then Taliesin sees Hooper's mutilated hand.

'Give him Class Assembly,' he says. 'He can tell us how he lost his finger in that tractor accident.' Taliesin thinks that this isn't a bad compromise for Hooper. It's a lush idea.

Hooper tenses and bores two holes in the back of Taliesin's brain with his stare. Hooper would rather do book collection for a term. Telling a story would be difficult; it might show him up.

'I'll kill you, Worm. I'll put this through your nose.' Hooper points the compass at him and makes the appropriate gestures with the instrument.

Just for a fraction Taliesin thinks that Hooper looks vulnerable. He looks like he has a mother and father who love him, kiss him good night and allow him to keep the landing light on.

'All right, all right. Quiet. Hooper, you will tell your story for the next Class Assembly.'

Hooper's mouth is beginning to quiver. 'But Sir.' (It's 'Sir' now.)

'No arguing.'

Hooper skulks back to his desk thinking of revenge. With focused skill he begins to stencil something into his desk.

There is slight trepidation in the class. Although David has subdued Goliath, someone has to pay. Conspiratorial whispers pass around the room.

'Hoop is going to go mental.'

'It wasn't my idea.'

'No, mine neither.'

'It was Worm's idea.'

'Worm is in for it now.'

'Yeah, Worm is in the shit.'

Mr Davies picks up the tatty registration book and holds it to his chest. 'Wait here for Mrs Philips.'

As soon as the teacher is out of the door Hooper strides over to Taliesin and locks him in a half-nelson.

'Sneak. Worm. "Tell a story . . . tell a story . . ." You little worm.' Hooper's grip tightens.

'I was only tryin' to help. It's better than writing "I must not flick Tanner's ear" one hundred times.' Hooper slackens his stranglehold a little.

'You Worm.'

'But it's easy Hoop. You can tell us about your finger. It will be ace.'

'There's nothin' to tell.'

'Yeah there is. Make it up. No one will know.' Hooper contemplates this suggestion. Embellishment shouldn't be a problem for him. Lying comes easy to Hoop. 'Just say what happened and add some extra stuff . . . I don't know . . . mention blood . . . that's interesting,' Taliesin goes on. Hooper almost smiles at the mention of blood. 'Tell us about your screaming. Loads of screaming. Tell us about scream-ing.'

Hooper lets go of his captive's shirt altogether. Taliesin rubs his neck and continues to encourage. 'You could draw a picture on the blackboard, explaining how it happened.'

By wriggling from the grip of the bully, Worm is living up to his name – one of its meanings at least. And the bully, bamboozled by brain, lollops back to his desk, lost in rare thought, looking at his finger-that-was and remembering blood.

During Biology Taliesin asks Mrs Philips why people get warts.

'From asking too many questions,' is her very unscientific answer. The biology textbook sheds no light on the answer either. The section on disease talks about Beriberi, Malaria, Smallpox and Yellow Fever and where you can catch them if you want them. During Geography, Taliesin asks Mr Gleason about Indian Summer and how long it will last.

'Strictly speaking an Indian Summer starts in October. But this weather won't last,' he adds. 'There's rain in the air.' And the geography teacher sniffs it. The class draw atolls, lagoons and the formation of volcanoes while Taliesin picks his own atoll at the end of his finger.

The final lesson before lunch is RE. Clouds must have drifted across the sun because the room is dark. It isn't Mr Tower who walks in but a new teacher who introduces herself as Miss Hamilton. Apparently Mr Tower is ill and Miss Hamilton is a student teacher standing in for Mr Tower while he is convalescing, which sounds worse than being ill.

'What's he got, Miss?'

'Will he be ill for ages, Miss?'

'Hope it's serious.'

Taliesin finds himself wishing that he'd sat nearer the front. The former teacher's obsession with church architecture had driven him to the back of the classroom where he would read rather than draw clerestories and crockets, fan vaulting and misericords. The gaunt and aquiline Mr Tower presided over a dark age of RE, but his replacement promises a dawning of a new age; an age of beauty and light. She might even be able to verify the truth of the Adam and Eve story.

Miss Hamilton distributes a leaning tower of crisp new exercise books – grey for RE. The unused book always offers Taliesin a chance to start again and put the poor presentation of the last book behind him. He can fill the white lined space with beautiful blotted answers. As he writes, he imitates the mature lean and curl of his mother's handwriting, taking particular care over his name.

The new teacher is waiting for the noise to settle, which in time it does more out of curiosity for a new face than respect. After introducing herself, Miss Hamilton sits side saddle on the desk, very relaxed.

'I'd like to start with a general discussion. That way I can get to know your names,' she says. 'You can keep your books closed and your pens down.' Taliesin screws the lid of his fountain pen back on. 'I'd like to begin by talking about our subject: RE. Can anyone tell me why we study RE?'

No one says anything. The class are much better at talking when they aren't asked to. Asking them something is a sure way to silence them.

'Well, let me ask you a slightly different question. What is RE? Can anyone tell me that?'

There are a few cheap-laugh answers muttered before Julie Dyer speaks. Julie Dyer is never wary of initiating things.

'It's to do with religion, Miss. Learnin' all about religion.'

'Good. Perhaps you could give me your names as you answer.'

'Julie Dyer, Miss.'

'I think that's a good answer, Julie. What else is it about? Someone else . . . yes, that boy there at the back.'

'Is it about God, Miss?' Taliesin disguises his answer as a question.

'What is your name?' she asks.

'Taliesin Jones.'

'Taliesin,' she mulls his name as people do. 'Yes. You could say that it is a study of how, what and why people believe in God.'

'Does that mean that if you don't believe in God then you don't have to do RE?' Hooper breaks in.

For a novice, Miss Hamilton handles him well.

'There are many people who study RE without necessarily believing in God,' she says.

'But no one believes in God anymore,' Hooper points out.

'I'm not sure that's true,' she counters. 'I'm sure some of you believe.'

'I bet you we don't,' Hooper says.

'Well, why don't we find out?' Miss Hamilton says. 'In

fact, that might be an interesting exercise.' There is both laughter and consternation at this approach.

'Let's start with those who believe in God? All right, all those who believe in God raise your hands. One, two, three, five . . . eight . . . eight. Any more?' Having seen this response one or two more put up their hands, including Luc Daniel. Taliesin is pleased to see his friend's hand hover agnostically for a time and then commit. Taliesin assesses his fellow voters. He has to acknowledge that the group is composed of the less fashionable elements of the class, except perhaps for the earthy Julie Dyer. 'Now all those who don't believe . . . one . . . two . . . four . . . six . . . eight . . . ten . . . twelve . . . twelve.' The atheist vote wins. Hooper leans back triumphantly, satisfied that his is the majority view.

The new teacher writes the statistics up on the board. 'If I was asking this same question to a class of children a hundred years ago, most of you would have said that you did believe. And perhaps in a hundred years time from now you would all say you didn't believe. It would be fascinating to see.'

'I think I gave the wrong answer, Miss,' William Jones says. 'Can I change?'

'There is no right and wrong answer,' the new teacher says. 'You can vote "not sure" if you want.'

Taliesin finds it disconcerting that he is in the minority. The existence of God is not something he has questioned. God has always been there since the beginning of the spiral in his atlas, long before people were around to vote as to whether God existed or not. Even now as he thinks about it he has a sense of God watching. He sees a pair of hands coming out of clouds; protecting, reprimanding, encompassing. The hands are mighty but strangely specific and human, with lines and marks. They are parting clouds and letting beams of light through. Don't the others see the same? He thought they did.

Confident that she has won the class over, the new teacher continues to push the children into thinking about why they voted the way they voted.

'You could say that RE is finding out where our beliefs come from. Why, for instance, did some of you say you believed in God and others not?' she says.

'They only believe because their parents do,' Hooper says.

'Rubbish. I made up my own mind, twerp,' Julie Dyer glowers.

Luc Daniel has his hand up. 'My parents don't believe in God. They say he's made up,' he says.

'They might be right,' the teacher says.

'Why don't you believe?' she asks Hooper, 'is it because of your parents?'

'I'm not believing in something I can't see,' Hooper says. When it comes to Taliesin to answer his thoughts blur and he is unable to articulate his feelings. He cannot account for his belief and its origins.

'I just do,' is all he can muster. This draws a ripping, derisory laugh from Hooper.

'That's no answer!' he roars.

Taliesin knows that it is no answer but his mind fails him, offering only vague suggestions which even in his head sound feeble. He feels protective towards the God he believes in and yet he doesn't know why. His loyalty certainly doesn't come from his parents. His mother used to go to chapel and sing. She liked to sing. But that was years ago. His father has always said he didn't need to believe. He believed what he wanted to believe. It was an aunt who gave him the *Illustrated Bible*, not his parents. He still says the same prayer that he said in primary school: Lord keep us safe this night secure from all our fears, may angels guard us while we sleep 'til morning light appears, Amen. He's continued to whisper the prayer to himself every evening, believing it to be received and acknowledged.

Julie Dyer and Hooper have started to argue. There is a great power struggle going on between them. Neither of them wants to concede anything to the other; too much is at stake.

The rest of the class all want to say why they do or don't believe and this causes the noise level to rise further. Meanwhile, Taliesin contemplates a new question. His mind is a maelstrom of divine polemic and it hurts his head. In moments of uncertainty he usually retreats to the safe haven of his imagination, a place where he is master of his thoughts and beliefs; a realm where he is emperor of eloquence. But even there he cannot escape the vast curling of a question that he never thought he'd have to ask.

During lunch break Taliesin takes his satchel to The Tall Tree in the corner of the playing field. The tree is an expansive thick-girthed oak, set apart from the grass on a bank which is raised up. It provides an unbroken view of the whole school. The leaves of The Tall Tree are a crisp brown and in the sunlight they appear to glow like fire. The tree's bark is covered in graffiti of mixed art and wisdom. These carvings give a potted history of the school's loves and hates: John 4 Juliet; Phil for me; Piss up a tree; Caesar eats Pizza. Maybe in a few years time, Taliesin will be carving in his name next to someone else's. For now he's happy to be single.

He takes the Cox's from his bag and shines the skin on his jumper. He whispers the greengrocer's aphorism to himself: 'Have an apple; go to chapel.' It has a natural rhythm and rhyme; the first line leading inevitably to the second. He turns the phrase over in his head and eventually says it out loud. 'Have an apple; go to chapel.' It's like a piece of advice a grandmother would give – it's old and it's wise and it's dotty. He understands the first part; the second however, makes little sense. Chapel is a strange place that exists for reasons he hasn't questioned.

Taliesin thinks of Eve again and tries to put himself in her naked soles. What if God hadn't said anything about not eating the apple? He sees Eve moving about the Garden Of Eden filling a basket with apples and then eating them until she makes herself sick. The Eve in his head is definitely his mother now.

Running feet come. It's Luc Daniel, panting from running for no reason. His blue, Aertex shirt is hanging out: Luc The Shirt. Taliesin pre-empts his friend by offering him a bite of the Cox's. They sit in silence for several minutes, sharing the apple. When they finally speak it is evident that they're thinking about the same thing.

'Why don't your parents believe in God, then?' Taliesin asks his friend.

'My Da says believing in God causes more trouble than good. Like that war in wherever it is. Do your parents believe in God then?' Luc asks.

Taliesin would like to think they do.

'Of course they do,' he lies, feeling that someone is watching him.

'Why do you believe in him?' Luc asks.

'I don't know,' Taliesin says, angry that he can't explain it again. Feeling suddenly cold he looks up at the sky and sees more clouds arriving to end the summer. How fickle the weather is. And how fragile his morning certainty.

CHAPTER FOUR

❧

In the afternoon Welsh Rain returns as if from a long holiday where it has replenished itself. Bulbous thunderheads roll in on all sides and position themselves for a downpour directly above the school. By three-thirty the first droplets splatter onto the hot road as he runs for his bus. They make an acrid limey smell on the tarmac, a smell that he can taste. Children run out of the main gate screaming and cheering as the first rumble breaks. Some parents sit in steaming cars with lights on and engines running, their wipers taking futile swipes at the rain which is now smacking onto all things without prejudice. A group of huddled mothers look vulnerable beneath their flimsy umbrellas. Taliesin sees 'Caesar', the headmaster, skipping across the front entrance with a newspaper over his head. The thunderstorm is a great leveller. No respecter of rank or importance, it splashes on teachers, parents and children in equal measure. The thunderstorm makes light of everything else that is going on, forcing people to notice things outside themselves and bow to something that they have no control over.

The cream and burgundy liveried bus chugs and growls at the stop. By the time Taliesin reaches it he can feel the rain trickling down inside his collar. Other wet children shake out their hair and laugh at what the rain has done to their clothes. 'Coach', the driver, seems unconcerned by the weather, sitting in his seat smoking while the bus fills with hysterical children. He leans on the big steering wheel and smirks at the panic. Coach likes to hurl the vehicle around corners with impressive force. Many young boys who ride with him want to be coach drivers, believing that they'll become like Coach: unafraid of thunderstorms and able to smoke and drive at the same time. From behind, he is like a thick silver milk urn leaning on the back of a trailer, looking as if he'll topple off his seat when the corners come, which they do with great frequency on this journey. His eyes flash in the huge interior rear mirror looking for trouble.

The journey from Prescelli to Cwmglum is a mere six miles and yet it takes some twenty-five minutes. Enough time to break the back of a good book. In twenty-five minutes Taliesin can usually get through a chapter and he has the ability to read in the vehicle without feeling sick. As he makes his way to his seat he reaches for his book.

Julie Dyer is already at the back. She has removed her jumper and let out her hair in order to comb the rain out with her hand. Whole rain drops sit on her thick luxuriant locks. In the year that Taliesin has travelled by bus Julie Dyer has grown almost-breasts which now press against her wet white blouse. He has followed their progress with interest and speculated with Luc Daniel as to their eventual size. Her confidence has grown in proportion to their growth. She has become an intimidating voluptuary, with a good heart. She lights up a cigarette, blows the smoke into her satchel and shoots him a salacious look. This is the girl who said she believed in God.

He tries to read his book. The animals, led by the pigs, have decided to get rid of the farmer and Taliesin is just thinking that it's a relief his father farms sheep when Julie nudges him.

'Do you wanna puff, Worm?'

He looks at the cigarette in her hand for a second or two before answering, 'No thanks.' He tried once but it didn't work out. The smoke caught in his throat and he gained little pleasure from it. It takes practice, he knows, but he doesn't want to humiliate himself in front of Julie Dyer. Julie is a professional; she doesn't cough or splutter as she smokes, she breathes it in and blows it out through her nostrils like the breath from a dragon. She makes cigarettes look good for you.

She is watching him now, thinking things he can't guess. Despite her overwhelming physicality he feels an affinity towards her. She was one of the ten who put up their hand with him in RE. Julie Dyer definitely would have plucked the apple had she been Eve. And she would not have hidden her shame when God reprimanded her. Julie Dyer is afraid of nothing. 'Julie Dyer, Julie Dyer, take me higher and higher,' the refrain goes. Her name alone conjures up imagery of temptation and initiation. She was the first girl to smoke, the first girl to have breasts, the first girl to beat boys racing. Taliesin is out of his depth even thinking about her, let alone talking to her. But she is kind to him, perceiving him with a certain fascination, without fear or threat. When she calls him 'Worm' it is with affection.

'Hey Worm, what you got there?' she asks.

'It's just a book,' he says.

'I hate books,' she says. 'I get so bored.' She leans in to take a closer look. 'What's it about?'

Taliesin loses his place.

'Hey, what's it about?' she asks, nudging him again. For a second Taliesin can't remember what it's about, he hasn't been concentrating at all.

'It's about these animals that decide to kill the farmer,' he says.

She looks at him and puffs out some smoke like an actress. 'Sounds a bit far-fetched. Is it any good?'

'So far.'

'I dunno how you can read in the bus. It makes me feel sick. Read me a good bit.'

She puts out the cigarette in the ashtray and ties her hair

back with her hands, pulling it into a bunch with a rubber band. She must be Spanish with all of that dark hair; Spanish or French, maybe.

'There's no point in reading a bit; you won't know what's going on. I'd have to explain everything to you,' Taliesin says.

'I don't mind, just read me a bit – any bit. Read me the bit when they kill the farmer – the animals.' She moves in close enough for him to smell her smoky, damp cardigan. One of the boys in the seat in front looks over the back of the headrest.

'Do I have to?' Taliesin pleads.

'Go on, just a page,' she says.

Reluctantly Taliesin starts to find the page where the animals kill the farmer. He reads it out in a flat monotone, trying to make it sound dull. But Julie is attentive. When he gets to the end of the passage she is hanging on his every word.

'Urgh. That gives me the creeps,' she says. 'What happens then?' Taliesin closes the book at the end of the chapter feeling self-conscious about reading out loud. The boys in front keep looking over the back of the seat at him, grinning stupidly.

'I'll read you some more tomorrow,' he says, putting the book in his satchel. She looks older with her hair back; more Grown-Up. She is looking at him again, going over his face with her eyes. He now wishes he hadn't put the book away. He wants to get away from her and he wants to be next to her and the two desires fight within him. Her brazen proximity both pushes him away and draws him in. She holds a promise and a knowledge of something that he is yet to know.

'I liked the new teacher,' she says. 'She had nice nails, and a nice figure.' Julie holds out her chubby fingers and parts them for individual inspection. 'What do you think of my nails?'

'They're great,' Taliesin says, tactfully. Great energy and love have gone into those nails. The varnish is thick with several layers of shocking red.

'I want to scratch Hooper's eyes out,' she says. Her hand curls into a claw and the nails turn to talons. 'He believes in God, really. He was just showing off. He was just doing it for effect. I hate him.' This isn't entirely true. Her vehemence betrays too much concern for Hooper. There is a rumour that they have kissed.

'But you believe,' she says, and this is pleasing to her.

Taliesin would like to proclaim his belief to her but he still can't think of a good reason as to why he believes, other than that he just does. He thinks about telling Julie about the hands in his book: the protecting hands, the admonishing hands, the healing hands, the creating hands – and almost does; but he can't quite bring himself to confide his particular vision, sensing that she might tear it to shreds with those claws. He stares at the seat cover in front of him, still troubled by these things.

'Tss. You should have heard what bloody rubbish they were sayin',' she rants. 'Jason Ball said that we should look for God in space. Like He is in the sky or something. He's not just up in the sky. He's in people as well,' she says, planting a finger in the middle of her chest.

This sounds far-fetched, even more far-fetched than talking pigs planning a revolution. Taliesin hasn't taken his idea of God beyond 'the hands' yet. Meanwhile, Julie Dyer pushes out her chest and says that God is inside her. Her simple theology has complex implications. If God is inside people then does that mean that there is more of Him in fat tall people than small thin people; more God in Julie Dyer than him; more God in an elephant than a sparrow. And if God is in him, which part of him does He inhabit? And then there is the business with Hooper. How could she kiss Hooper and believe in God?

Coach calls out the stop. 'Read me some more tomorrow,' Julie Dyer says. She winks at him but he can't respond with anything more than a nod to the floor. The bus shudders impatiently as he gets off. Coach revs the engine, wanting to get moving, begrudging the stop. Taliesin is the only one for Cwmglum.

Outside the cloud has now lowered and become a grey oppressive weight. He holds his satchel over his head and walks behind the bus before crossing the road. He hears a tap at the back window and he sees Julie, her face pressed ugly against the glass, steaming it up with her breath. She makes a pig-like snorting motion and laughs. The pneumatic doors hiss shut and the bus drives on. The gargoyle girl grins and recedes in the drear.

Taliesin wishes he'd worn the jumper that his mother had given him for his birthday, the one with lanolin. And he should have worn his mack. It is much cooler now and the rain more spiteful. Clouds arrive and puncture on the high hills and mountains of Wales, forming a layer of billowing architecture, beneath which the rain comes down in cascades, trying to match the feats of rain in deepest darkest Africa or the rainforests of South America. This rain would make dark purple on the rainfall chart in his atlas. He sees the rain coming down, showing off, full of confidence, strutting in sheets. Welsh Rain is enthusiastic and generous. It wants to make sure everyone and everything has some. It tops up lakes and swells rivers, cleans the roads, soaks the old woman's hat, kisses bulbs, gets in socks, embraces dryness like a long lost friend. It baptises notes in milk bottles, drenches trees; it finds the cat's milk saucer and the small of a boy's back.

Through the gloom Taliesin can see his home, see his father's sheep, slightly luminous in the dark fields. Thankfully they are too stupid to think up anything as clever as 'Four legs good, two legs bad.' He can see where the fields pour together and form a valley, the farmhouse and its squat outhouses, the figures of his brother and dog moving across the field towards the house, the dog weaving in and around imaginary sheep mapping out a figure of eight.

The farmland is a patchwork of grey-browns and grey-greys, spreading out like a dour quilt covering a fat king in his bed. Farm houses, slate-roofed and slanting in the rain, stitch the edges of the chequered landscape together. The slate roofs have many hues. They can be purple-bluish like mussel shells or green like the sea, or just plain grey.

The lane to his house is half a mile long and hedgerows grow tall on either side. It rises and then falls and at the halfway point on top of the hill there is just enough light to see the farm outhouses and the purple fields beyond. In the fields the water irrigates the summer earth, turning everything to mud. A lightning fork illuminates the panorama for a second, framing it in electric blue, and only a second later Heaven rumbles. In this half light the blackberry bushes, cow parsley, pink campion and dandelions are no longer flowers. Their brilliance loses its identity in black. The rain paints everything the same colour.

At this cross-over time of day things blur and become other things. Bushes curl into triffids, leaves flicker warnings, and there is always someone behind him, sniggering at the passing of the light.

Taliesin walks fast without showing fear to any who might be looking. If he met something along this path there would be no escape. But despite the rain he mustn't run because then his fear would only follow him faster. He must walk quickly but calmly and try to focus on 'normal' things; things so mundane that even the creatures that thrive in a lively mind are not stirred. He thinks about pencil sharpeners and maths, but somehow the pencil sharpeners are too sinister, too suggestible. He thinks about his mother but somehow that brings him to snakes. He thinks about sheep but that only leads him back to pigs.

He starts to run through the rain trying in vain to dodge the million water arrows. He thinks he can hear pigs running upright on their hind legs chanting, 'Four legs good, two legs bad', – that book is getting to him. Even as he runs the dark descends. He can no longer distinguish the sky from the earth.

He wonders if God is angry. He wonders about God being in him. It seems that his childhood ideal of the parting out-spread hands of God is in need of updating and revision – like so many of his childhood ideals.

At this cross-over time of life things blur: what to believe, what not to believe; what to discard, what to keep; what to learn, what not to learn; what to read, what not to read; whether to be a child or a Grown-Up; whether to be afraid of the dark or not afraid. He can't imagine a time when he won't be afraid of the dark. He still leaves the door ajar at night enough to admit a thin eye of light from the landing. When he can sleep without the light from the landing he will know he's a Grown-Up.

His father's dog, Moss, smells him coming from a hundred yards away and starts to bark as if he were a burglar. At fifty yards Moss is straining at the chain and twisting himself in an effort to get to him. Only when he is close up does the animal stop its lunatic behaviour. Once it has recognized him it starts to wag its whole body and make ecstatic whimpering noises. Taliesin is wary of the dog's unpredictability; he finds it hard to trust animals at the moment and according to Mr Orwell dogs are only marginally more trustworthy than pigs.

'It's only me, Moss,' he says, like a tentative postman. He's never felt comfortable talking to animals, unlike his mother who can hold whole conversations with cats.

The certainty that he has felt all day ebbs away as he approaches his home. He slows as he comes into the outside light of the house. The rain that falls in front of the light is suddenly brilliant, flashing white. Rain is rivering down the slant of the roof, filling the guttering and over-spilling onto the front concrete. It splatters loudly and the spillage creates a moat about the house, like a castle. Not so long ago he called his house a castle. It was the centre of a kingdom whose laws and boundaries were unquestioned. All things were well in the kingdom and it seemed no evil could come to it. Then one day, the queen was offered a shining red apple in which she saw the reflection of the person she wanted to be. She realized that all this time she hadn't been herself, not happy at all. She only had to take the apple to be happy again. Although the laws of the kingdom forbade her to take the apple, its spell was too strong. She abdicated her throne and left the king and his two sons behind. And no one was sure of anything any more.

CHAPTER FIVE

THE EVENTS OF LAST YEAR linger around the rooms in petrified time. When Taliesin's mother left, the clocks in the house all stopped. It was she who set the pendulum swinging and it was always her who turned the key of the carriage clock that ticked a furious little tick on the mantlepiece in the sitting room. When she left she took time present and future with her, leaving time past and imperfect solidifying to stony tense memories. Since she left Taliesin has noticed her. He's even felt her presence more strongly than those who are still living in the house with him. In her absence he's been getting to know and appreciate her.

The coat rack tells him that his father has finished work on the farm and taken his corduroy jacket to the Golden Fleece. His work smock and jacket are recently hung and still wet. Taliesin's own forgotten anorak mocks him and reminds him that things can change very quickly, even in a day. His brother's boots and mack have been dumped on the floor, probably discarded in a hurry to catch a television pro-gramme. A silk headscarf belonging to his mother is draped on the end peg, no one daring to touch or acknowledge it. With this many absconders and escape artists under one roof, it is no surprise that the home has an empty feel to it.

It is quiet enough to hear the fridge going through the gears. The kitchen is a mess and it draws attention to itself. With a mother around the family were protected from the decay and the dust and the build up of refuse. Now these things conspire and make themselves known. Even the electric cabling, something he's never noticed before, looks exposed and dangerous. The top of the fridge has a thin film of grime and the cat's saucer has become sculpted to the surface by neglect. The lack of a mother discloses all kinds of things to his eyes, nose and ears. There is no longer a smell of things she might have cooked or sprayed on; nor the sight of things she might have used, nor the colour of things she might have cleaned, nor the sound of her voice insulating against this uncomfortable quiet. These things he took for granted and being taken for granted was a thing she hated – along with not having enough colour in her life.

He tries to picture his mother and is shocked that he can't remember what she looks like – his own mother and he can't picture her! It's like a film where a man hits his head on a rock and knocks himself out. When he wakes he can remember very specific details, such as the name of his mother's perfume and the way she curled her S's; but he can't remember what she looked like. Taliesin pulls the scarf from the end peg and presses it to his nose. From it he creates a composite of her, the way that a bloodhound might pick up the trail of an escapee from the scent of a torn cloth. The scarf's softness is cool and its scent projects her image into his mind: her long elegant nose that on other faces might be too big; her brown and slow-blinking eyes; a low forehead and slightly rounded, always powdered cheeks. In this mind's-eye portrait she has the scarf on, covering her hair, then she pulls the scarf away and her hair spills out with a fulsome bounce. The hair isn't quite how he remembers it. She has changed her style. Her hair has been cut in a way that makes her look younger; cut by someone who thinks she looks better that way. And she thinks she looks better that way. She is saying so now, like the woman in the shampoo advertisement: 'I feel like a new woman.' Behind her there is sea and rows of colourful houses lining the shore.

West Haven: that's where she went to get her hair done.

Twice a year she went there to shop and get her hair cut by 'Toni': Toni Phillips, the hairdresser. It was her 'one extravagance' she said, her 'big treat'. And when she returned she was radiant and a little flushed. 'The air there is marvellous,' she'd explain.

Then one day, a year ago, she stayed there overnight and the carriage clock stopped through lack of winding. When she came back, his father told her that he didn't like the way her hair had been cut. 'Toni likes it this way,' she said. They then had an argument in which she did all the talking. She told his father that life on the farm was boring and that she was going to live in West Haven with Toni. She kept saying that she wanted a little more colour in her life and that she didn't like being taken for granted. She really hated being taken for granted. She said this as if someone had suddenly pointed it out to her. His father said nothing. He just stared at her as if on the verge of laughter and tears, his eyes wide at the sight of her. When he eventually spoke he just asked, 'How could you go and live with a man who spells Tony with an "i" at the end?'

That evening Taliesin's mother sat down with him and Jonathan and told them that she still loved them, and that she still loved their father too, but that she couldn't tolerate living with him any more. She said that it would be bad for everyone if she stayed at home being unhappy. She added that they would be better off on the farm with their father and going to the same school. It was important not to interrupt their schooling.

Her going was so low-key it seemed normal. The event had a comic clarity, a calmness that bore no relation to what was actually happening. No one knew what to say. Families don't get a chance to rehearse for these things. There are no rules for how they should conduct themselves. At the time, it was just another difficult day.

Taliesin clearly remembers their last meal together – his

mother wouldn't sit down. She insisted that she cook them all supper and make the tea and she then apologized for the tea being too weak. It came out all piss yellow and under-brewed, the way she liked it and the way Taliesin's father hated it. Taliesin's father put more tea bags into the pot and burnt his fingers. His mother then got up and held his father's hand under the cold tap, soothing the burn. She was going but she could still do this.

Taliesin's mother continued to apologize for everything – the tea, the burn, the way she'd done the eggs. His father started to enthuse about his latest plan; a plan guaranteed to put more colour in all of their lives. He talked in assumptives, as if nothing had happened and that everything was all right, which it clearly wasn't. His father always brought up his plans when things around him were going ill.

The next morning they helped their mother pack a hope-lessly small suitcase which was light enough for Taliesin to carry to the car. Jonathan stayed in his room and refused to come out; he locked his door and wouldn't let his mother in. She stood outside his room beseeching him to let her say goodbye properly, but Jonathan said nothing.

She said she didn't want to go but that she had to, as though driven by invisible forces beyond her control. She drove off with tears carving up her make-up. Her reluctance was enough to slow the car but not to stop it. Taliesin's father remained absurdly calm, insisting that she take the car as though she were just going off to the shops or something. As she drove away he began to laugh, saying that she'd only packed one pair of knickers and would have to come back.

After a week Taliesin thought it was about time she came back for some more knickers. His father conceded that West Haven was full of knicker shops and that she must have purchased a whole load of new ones. Then his father told them that their mother was going to stay in West Haven for 'a little longer', to sort some things out and put more colour in her life. Taliesin and Jonathan could see her whenever they wanted to, at weekends and during the holidays.

His father didn't seem that upset, just numb. He was unable to respond in a dramatic fashion, looking always as if he had something else on his mind, which he did. Occasionally at meal times (which began to consist of baked beans and fish fingers) he would shake his head gently and mumble the name 'Toni' incredulously. Apart from that he hardly said anything about the subject and continued to behave as though their mother would soon be back from her prolonged shopping trip.

Taliesin expected the walls to come tumbling down but they didn't. Life went on. According to people at school it wasn't that odd to have separated parents. Apparently it was normal, like measles; and apparently there were benefits like receiving twice as many presents at Christmas.

His father escaped to his head. He began to talk to himself and he could be heard arguing it all through. He had his plans to fall back on. Now he could indulge his pipe dreams, inhale their heady vapour and let them carry him away to Eldorado. He had always talked about moving, giving it all up and doing something different. The schemes recurred according to the season. Winter was thick with plans, often a different one a week. They were like fanciful tales or fables and he told them well and made his listeners believe in him. The fables all had the same fantastic implausibility and the same ending. There was the plan to sell the farm to an Englishman with a fat wallet and a gun dog, or an Arab with twelve wives and an oil well, or an American looking for a country retreat. Then he wanted to buy a clipper with four sails and a Plimsoll line and sail for the Indies where it was too hot to wear wool. And there was the plan to move to America. He made them all look at maps and choose places they liked the sound of – Nantucket, Elmore, Mount Moon, even Eldorado itself. When Taliesin's mother left, his father was obsessed with one particular scheme which he insisted had possibility. But of course it was too late. Taliesin's mother had grown accustomed to the latest idea, grown bored of choosing nice sounding names from a map, become fed up with talk of Spice Islands, ranches and tropical promise. She wanted a real place to escape to, somewhere that was easy to find.

Jonathan took it badly, which was a surprise to Taliesin because his brother didn't seem to care about anything much except sport and television. He reacted by watching more sport on television, finding a form of escape in its endless minutiae and statistics. He moped and sat in a sullen heap in the same chair in front of the screen, the images flickering on his saturnine face, making little impression on his expression. It was as if a draught from the door had set his face into a permanent grimace. When he spoke it was with an accusative glower and invariably directed towards his mother, who he now referred to as 'her' or 'she'.

Taliesin also escaped to his head. There he could couch these events in storybook terms. His mother was the queen who was bewitched; his father a king who talked to himself; his brother a prince who forgot laughter. Books also provided an easy refuge. There he could disengage himself from the complications of his own life. He sought books that carried him away for days, where the dramas of the fictional world became as real or more real than his own, and where his own problems were as nothing compared to the heroic disasters and catastrophes which befell the characters he read about.

Jonathan's two-legs-good are on the stool and his piggy eyes are on the television. Since he left school he's grown a little fatter from watching rather than playing sport. He still has the arrogance of health and the natural grace of the athlete – having inherited all the right genes for these things – but his dispirited demeanour ruins nature's good work. He would be handsome if he smiled a bit. But nothing makes him smile these days. Blanking the idea of his mother's existence requires concentration and resolute determination.

When Taliesin enters the sitting room he gets no greeting from Jonathan who sees saying hello to his younger brother as beneath him. The only way for Taliesin to communicate successfully with his brother is to find a lowest common denominator like sport or food. Conversation with him is rarely a continuous flow of dialogue, never more than a series of questions and answers.

'Do you want some toast?' Taliesin asks.

Jonathan keeps his eyes on the screen and gives a slow nod. The programme he is watching is swinging from mood to mood: a girl is laughing, a woman is crying, someone is dying and then someone is laughing. None of this mood change seems to register on Jonathan's blank face.

In the kitchen Taliesin puts two slices into the toaster and lights the Raeburn, amazed that he is lighting a fire on a day that began so warmly. He spreads the Marmite taking no notice of the maker's instructions to spread thinly. By the time he returns to the television the programme has finished. Jonathan concedes a thank you for the toast and eats it uncut. Taliesin neatly dissects his into four squares, analysing and savouring each piece, taking care to miss nothing.

The news starts and the world offers up its events. A tank drives at high speed through a desert and a reporter stands at the end of the picture with wind blowing his hair.

Jonathan clears his throat.

'She wants to know what you're doing for Christmas. She said she'll ring again next week some time.'

His brother passes on this information hurriedly. Jonathan has not seen his mother since closing his bedroom door and locking it the morning she drove off. Since then he's worked hard at occluding her from his life. These telephone calls undermine his vigilance.

'Are you going to go?' Taliesin asks.

'Am I fuck. Spend Christmas with that poncy bastard?' Taliesin's own swearing is fledgling and experimental and Jonathan's words shock: the words themselves, their vehemence and the fact that they're unjust.

'You haven't met him yet. He's not so bad.'

'I don't need to know.' It is helpful to Jonathan's cause that his mother has an accomplice, and therefore someone else to blame. He has already decided that he doesn't like Toni, whatever he's like. Taliesin can tell that in Jonathan's imagination Toni is dark, has an evil grin, rakish smile, fast car, gold chain, plush carpets, and is as vain as he is tanned: the Wicked Stepfather.

Taliesin will have to go there for Christmas alone.

'I think I should go,' he says.

'It's your funeral.'

Jonathan lifts his whole body off the chair with his arms, holding his legs in midair for a second, his stomach taking the strain. Jonathan expresses himself this way, with his body.

'It might be okay . . . at Christmas,' Taliesin limply encourages.

'Who needs it? I certainly don't.' Standing, Jonathan is six feet and he may yet grow another two inches. He saunters from the room self-consciously setting his face into a frown and leaves, perhaps to meet his new girl at the Fleece.

Taliesin stays and watches the screen. There is already talk of Christmas. It is luring him from a long way off, with its dual promise of presents. Seventy shopping days, says The Man On The Telly; seventy days for his mother to buy him something, and seventy days for his father to match her. Competition improves things, they say. After the news The Man On The Telly confirms that all good things must come to an end and that Indian Summer has now given way to Welsh Rain.

He can hear his mother now telling him to do things: to

43

clear the tea things away, to dry his hair and change out of his damp things, to go and practise the piano. She has left a busy and bossy ghost behind in her place. Taliesin returns the tea things to the kitchen and finishes his toast by the Raeburn. He can feel the Marmite stinging an ulcer in his mouth. Through the Raeburn window the flames eat their way through the wood which cracks and spits in submission. The mild smells of toast and woodsmoke remind him of Christmas.

He continues to heed his mother's voice and goes to the dining room. The piano, its sound and the thing itself, reminds him of his mother. She was at her most attractive when she sat here on the stool, her back arching and her head swaying with the playing. He feels close to her when he's sitting on the embroidered seat that lifts up and contains sheets of music; classical scores and carols that she would play every year while he held and turned the pages.

His music book is still open at the piece he hasn't practised. 'A Dancing Bear' sits there on the stand looking difficult and unplayable. He must practise it in time for Saturday when he will walk to a bungalow the other side of the village and sit for an hour with Billy Evans, his piano teacher. He'll play the piece through (by ear) pretending to sight read – something he has successfully done for six months, concealing his musical dyslexia by getting Billy to play it through and trying to memorize the piece. His talent was promising enough to be encouraged, but it's insufficient to breeze things without effort. His ear, he is told, is good, but his eye and the mechanism that transforms the notes on the page to the movement of the fingers at the right speed and pressure isn't. Unlike the words in a book, notes don't translate quickly and clearly in his head and he suspects that his teacher already knows this and is simply too kind to expose the fact.

Taliesin started his piano lessons when his mother's hair was still getting fresh attention and his father's plans were

44

getting fancy. Piano wasn't something he chose to do. His mother wanted one of her children to play the piano and Jonathan's early sporting prowess ensured that it was Taliesin who had to be musical. He agreed to do it because he imagined himself playing tunes as easily as he could play them in his head. He hadn't anticipated the science of it.

Things began well. His learning curve rose sharply and quickly and the early success gave him an enthusiastic momentum, which for a time overcame the fundamental problem. Then the curve peaked into a flat straight line when he realized that he couldn't read the notes. His mother wasn't around to give him a hand. Before she left, she found him a teacher in the village. Taliesin was his only pupil. Were it not for Billy he would have stopped having the lessons altogether. Thankfully his teacher is patient, never raising his voice in anger or frustration at his pupil's obvious lack of progress, always turning failing into attribute, seeing only the good.

He tries to play 'The Dancing Bear' but he can't string it together. He starts to twiddle around the keyboard, playing the little tunes he knows by heart. He plays these with the swagger of a confident virtuoso, imitating his mother's sway. It's easier to stick to things he knows and let himself believe that he is actually quite good. He always indulges the same fantasy at the piano, flicking imaginary tails from underneath him, acknowledging the applause and using plenty of loud pedal.

After a while he has to stop to examine his hands. At the end of his index finger another wart is growing. He can feel it as he presses the keys. This wart is a lighter colour than the original and already larger. He starts to pick at it, holding the finger between his thumbs seeing how much pressure he can apply before he feels pain. Perhaps the teacher is right after all — warts are caused by lying and he has lied about his ability to read music. He feels the need to scrub his hands.

In the bathroom he lathers up the soap more than he needs to and washes his hands as if trying to hide evidence. He resolves to tell Billy Evans everything before his next lesson. When he dries his hands, he sees that the hand towel is filthy. Someone hasn't rinsed their hands properly and they've used it to wipe off the dirt. No wonder he has warts. No one is providing clean laundry in this place. The bathroom is not as sweet smelling as it was. The windowsill that once displayed his mother's ablutive creams, lotions and potions is empty except for his father's silver razor and Jon's cheap aftershave and Bics.

Taliesin hears the front door open and the deep trumpet of his father's voice.

'Helloo?'

Taliesin takes the dirty towel and puts it in the laundry basket. His father has eased his broad frame into a wooden chair which creaks under his weight. At a glance he is no more Taliesin's father than Adam. He is dark and his colouring lends him a fierce air, like some South Walian Heathcliff, a description which is accentuated by a permanent shadow. His full head of wiry black hair is the texture of Brillo-pad and when it rains the droplets sit on it as they do now. His nose is thick and passionate and his eyebrows have a flourishing life of their own and run in one continuous bushy line from one side of his head to the other. This lupine effect is softened by the eyes, the same mahogany saucer eyes as Taliesin's; searching, enthusiastic eyes with a naive expectancy.

'How was school?' he asks, mustering a smile and then staring away beyond Taliesin at the fridge and the cat's saucer.

'Okay,' Taliesin says.

'That's good. Did Jonathan mention your Mam ringing?'

Taliesin nods.

'Don't feel that you have to stay here for Christmas. It's her turn to have you.' He says this as if he's rehearsed it.

Taliesin fingers an old newspaper article on holidays.

'Will you go then?' his father asks.

'I don't mind.' Taliesin isn't sure what to say.

'As long as you don't think I mind. She's still your mother.'

In his head Taliesin sees his mother with nothing on in a garden with Toni. They're picking all types of apples and have trotters instead of legs.

His father has been drinking. His smile is unnatural and his clothes give off a pungent pub smell. He has started going to the Golden Fleece regularly these last few months; 'catching a few drinks' when he's finished on the farm. Taliesin has walked past the pub on his way to school and wondered what goes on in it. The painted sign hanging above the entrance depicted a golden fleece that looked more like a manky anorak than an odyssey inducing trophy. Jason and his Argonauts wouldn't have bothered. The 'Children Not Allowed' notice only made him more suspicious.

His father leans in conspiratorially.

'I've got something exciting to tell you. I don't want you to breathe a word of it to anyone. Don't say anything to Jonathan. And don't tell your mother yet. I want it to be a surprise. It's all right. I know what you're thinking,' he says. 'I know, I know. But. Listen. Listen to me. I've been talking to a man about the cave. We could open it to the public. Stalactites. Stalagmites. Of course, I'll need to talk to the authorities first – get it checked – but I can't see that there would be a problem.'

His father has been talking himself into this idea for a while. He first mentioned it a year ago. Taliesin's mother said she thought it a mad idea. He insists it is his most realistic and straightforward yet; that the cave might be of interest to the public. Since his mother left home, Taliesin has noticed how his father talks to him in a different way, not as a father might talk to a son, more as a husband might talk to a wife. It is as though he is looking for the approval he failed to get. He knows that Taliesin will listen to his plans without undermining them.

'Is it safe?' Taliesin asks.

'We'd need lights and steps. Nothing that can't be done. I'll show it to you.' His father rubs his eyes, massages his temples and hums.

Taliesin looks at his parents differently these days. He once felt perfectly confident telling his friends how exemplary his mother and father were; how clever his father, how musical his mother, how utterly brilliant they generally were. But the myth is being exposed and he will have to find new pedestals for them to stand upon. Pedestals set at a lower, less dizzying altitude and made of something less than marble.

His father yawns and picks up a new line in an old way.

'You can take the train to West Haven, I think there's a train from Prescelli. We've got a timetable.' He gets up and rummages for a timetable in a drawer.

'I'm not going yet,' Taliesin says.

'Arrivals, arrivals . . . departures . . . here. Yes, straight through. You don't even have to change.' He leans forward and begins to rub his forehead. He looks up and out of the window, listening. 'Thank God it's raining,' he says.

Taliesin's mind is receptive to this.

'You believe in God, don't you?'

'I'm not sure that I do really,' his father says.

Taliesin is amazed at this confession.

'But you pray sometimes?' Taliesin asks.

'I used to. In the fields.'

'What did you say?'

His father begins to laugh.

'I don't know . . . anything. I usually just asked for something.'

'Did you get what you asked for?'

'It depends how you look at it. There's always the chance

that it was going to happen anyway. It doesn't always work. I'm not sure about it anymore. It gets tricky. I have my own belief. That gets me by. Anyway, why are you so interested in these things? You don't want to be worrying about all of that.'

His father is agitated. It may be that he's tired and finding it hard to think just now. Or it may just be that he doesn't like this topic of conversation. He must feel let down; punished for something he hasn't done. It wasn't him who took the apple. No wonder he isn't sure if he believes anymore.

Taliesin can't understand why God is such a grey area of uncertainty. Why some see God as clear as light and others see nothing but the dark. For some, it seems, God is made up, He can't be located, no one seems to have seen Him, He hasn't featured in the news. For others He is as real as an apple; He can be found in everything, even inside of us. Is there a right or wrong answer, or does it just depend? Is there a completely utterly categorical yes, or an absolutely totally definite no? He needs to know but it seems that no one has the answer.

CHAPTER SIX

❧

THINGS ARE ON HIS MIND as he walks to his piano lesson,
holding his score to his chest. He's been trying to step to the
3/4 rhythm of 'The Dancing Bear', but being a waltz it is
difficult. He tries the pat-a-cake pat-a-cake tempo of a tune
that he keeps hearing in the playground, a tune that girls skip
to:

> Underneath the arches and over the sea
> boom, boom, boom,
> I know that (Whoever it is) still waits for me
> boom, boom, boom.

But this isn't a tune to walk to. Finally he settles on the
rhythm of his intentions:

> I'm going to tell him,
> I'm going to tell him,
> I'm going to tell him,
> today.

Today, he will tell Billy Evans that he can't read a single
note of music and that for the last few months he has been
pretending to read the score whilst relying on his ear to get
him through. This is hard because he doesn't want to stop
having lessons. He likes Billy. In fact, he's never felt so
comfortable in the company of anyone. When he's with Billy
he feels a peace that he can't explain. He experiences none of

the usual age barriers that are rigidly maintained between children and adults. Billy must be seventy and yet Taliesin talks to him as though he were a playground friend, a fact which has made him all the more wretched about his deception.

Taliesin has sensed that his teacher knows about his inability to read music. It's as if Billy is waiting for him to admit it, rather than cruelly expose his failing. Indeed, there are times when Billy seems to know exactly what Taliesin is thinking. How often have his teacher's words trodden softly in the fresh prints of his thoughts?

Although he hardly reads books, Billy has the knack of seeing a thing. He is at once direct and sensitive, getting quickly to the root of meaning. He has few of the usual Grown-Up traits: evasion, deception, condescension. He never says, 'I told you so.' Billy has a gentle deference to things that happen, an acceptance that there is something more important than his own life. This is rare in Taliesin's eyes. Billy isn't rich – his house isn't even a whole house, his piano isn't priceless and he has no car. He isn't the cleverest man in Wales. He doesn't read many books, hadn't heard of *Animal Farm* and has never read 'The Elephant Child'. Billy even admits to not knowing the answer to things.

When Taliesin started his lessons he heard his father refer to his teacher as 'Evans The Touch'. Taliesin presumed this referred to Billy's way with the keys until his mother mentioned that Billy was a healer. Taliesin asked her what that was. She said something about Billy helping the sick, swiftly adding that Taliesin was not to ask Mr Evans about it because 'it was a very private matter. It was very good of Mr Evans to give up his time, so he mustn't be troubled with all sorts of questions.'

This was a gauntlet that he had to pick up. 'All sorts of questions' began to float to the surface. What exactly did Billy do when he healed people? How did he do it? Was it magic? Were there spells? Was he some kind of wizard? Was this something that Grown-Ups needed to keep a secret? Something they didn't want to talk about – like God? Who were these people who kept coming to his teacher's house after the piano lesson? Many times he had arrived for a lesson just as someone – clearly not well – was leaving the bungalow. And only last week an old lady sat in the lounge, bent over like a tree in the wind, her hand shaking as she stirred her tea, while Taliesin tried to play 'The Dancing Bear'. He wanted to ask Billy who she was and why she was there. She looked too old to be learning piano.

The vague explanations of his parents were not enough to sate his curiosity. If they couldn't explain what it was that Billy Evans did then he would find out for himself. Sooner or later he'd ignore his mother's instructions not to ask questions. To date this prohibition has kept him discreetly silent. But perhaps if he shares his own secret with Billy he will be in a position to ask him.

Welsh Rain has stopped for a rest and allows the land to drain off the recent fall. It leaves the air damp and cool.

> Rain, rain, go away,
> Come again another day.

Billy's bungalow has a prefabricated extension built around the doorway, acting as a porch. The roof here is corrugated plastic and translucent, so that when it rains it smacks on the cover and makes a din. The jerry-built front is filled with junk, including a piano without a lid, the white keys looking like teeth with gums pulled back. There are ladders, boots, some blue overalls, cutting equipment and a small pile of slate, left over from his days as a roofer. Although it's ugly, Taliesin likes Billy's home because it isn't a normal house. It has a temporary, toy-town feel, as if it's meant to be played in rather than lived in.

Billy is slow to come to the door and he looks tired and grey. Sleep dust dulls the twinkle in his eye and he is wearing a dressing gown over his clothes. He holds out an ushering hand and leads Taliesin into the warmth.

'It's stopped raining,' Taliesin says. Billy smiles his half smile. His movements are more languid than usual and his dressing gown gives him the air of the invalid. He pats his chest and emits a rasping cough.

'The weather's given me a chill,' he explains.

Taliesin is hot from his walk and his music book weighs twice what it did when he set off. Inside the bungalow it's stifling and the whole place smells of gas. The fire is on the full three bars and hissing its heat out. It gives the formica and plastic interior a faint orange glow. A chair is right up close to the fire and a blanket lies on the floor. Billy pulls up another chair for Taliesin and goes to the kitchen to put on the kettle.

'Two sugars is it?' Billy asks.

'Yes, please.'

Billy makes the tea with ritualistic attention to detail: warming the pot with a cupful of just-boiled water, adding the bags and water before placing a cosy over the pot and letting it stand for three minutes, putting the milk in the mugs and pouring the tea, the spout some twelve inches from the lip. It's the hands that Taliesin watches closely. Everything done with those hands has a sureness of touch and a calm beauty. The tea enters the cup with an exquisitely irritating noise and as the cup fills he lowers the pot towards it. Then he adds the sugars, stirring them vigorously before tapping the spoon dry, all the time smiling his smile.

Billy's face invites those who meet him to relax. It is the face of an ageless cherub with laughing eyes that blink and twinkle rapidly as if letting you in on a joke. Reverence and irreverence jostle for supremacy there but neither of them wins. Some smiles smile at things or with things, before and after things, some patronize, some anticipate. Billy's smile is a smile of gentle surprise at the wonder of it all; a smile that finds beauty in every little thing – even the stirring and tapping of a stainless steel teaspoon.

'I'm afraid we may have to cut the lesson short today,' he says. 'I don't know if you remember the lady who sat with us last week? She'll be turning up again today. It's the only time she can come. We'd better make a quick start.' Billy nods towards the piano.

When Taliesin first saw Billy's piano he was disappointed. He expected a piano teacher to own a piano of the highest quality – something German sounding and black. But compared to Taliesin's father Billy is poor. His house only has one floor and his piano sounds tinny compared to the full, rounded timbre of his mother's German, mahogany, one-hundred-year-old piano which she always described as priceless. Taliesin has yet to find out how much priceless is. Priceless is a word used to describe jewels found in chests by pirates. When he asked Billy Evans if his piano was priceless Billy replied that it was worthless. He owned nothing that was priceless, he said.

The room is sparsely decorated: a jubilee mug and a pipe rack with two pipes in it stands by the fire. Just above the television is a single shelf with a brass bell and a lilac figurine of a lady. On top of the television is a Bible thick enough to wind-break a chapel door. Billy used this book to improve Taliesin's posture at the piano. By balancing it on his head Taliesin was forced to sit correctly and he now sits well, thanks to the imagined presence of the book lying across his crown.

Taliesin starts to play 'The Dancing Bear', playing it as if he's reading the music. He isn't able to admit anything yet. He even feigns a squint.

'That's a little too fast,' Billy says. 'You need to let the gaps in. The gaps make the music work.'

Taliesin starts again, playing it more slowly, leaving more time between the bars.

'Those are pauses but they're not gaps. You're not feeling the gaps. Let me show you.' Billy plays the piece an octave up the keyboard. He is a robust man and this accentuates the delicacy with which he plays. His hands are wide and thick fingered. They have a weight, an aura, they possess an intelligence of their own. Taliesin's father always said that you could tell a lot from someone's hands: age, occupation, even personality. Billy's hands say a great deal. They are wide, hairless, mottled, generous hands, built to applaud life and restore it; hands that might clasp you on either shoulder and steer you in the right direction; working hands with battered half-moonless nails, chipped here and there; hands that you really noticed when they were still; old hands with a vivid glow; large veined, octave stretching hands with fingers that might occasionally strike two notes instead of one: praying, playing, laying hands.

Taliesin stares blankly at the music. The gaps are not formally indicated on the score; there are no curling G's or extra spaces to guide him.

'I don't know what you mean – about the gaps,' he says.

'They're the secret to it. Not just music. But everything else: talking, laughing, breathing. It's like a time in between something, when nothing happens and when you're not looking back or forward. The gaps make the things around them, either side, stand out.' Billy pauses and catches his breath before going on. 'So if I play a note like this . . . and I lift up my finger . . . and then play it again . . . you can hear that the gap is more important than the note. Without the gap the notes are just notes. Try it again.'

As Taliesin plays he can feel the wart at the end of his index finger. It has grown to the size of a pea in a matter of days and it hurts when he applies pressure to the key.

'Have a sip of your tea,' Billy says. 'I think we can leave

"The Dancing Bear". You know it well enough. You need a new piece to stir up your enthusiasm.'

Billy turns the page on the stand and a new piece sits there, untried, unheard, like some complex equation. It's called 'Bugles!' and Taliesin can only guess at its tune. He sees that the notes rise and fall but he cannot be sure of what they indicate. He simply can't understand this language of black dots. If only staffs, semibreves, clefs, bars and crotchets were like words in a book, then he'd play them. If only the notes made sounds the way that words made pictures, then he'd be a player. He can't work out the first note so he places a hopeful finger somewhere near the middle.

'That's a B,' Billy says, ever encouraging. 'One more up. C, that's it.'

The next note is higher up the lines so it could be an E or an F. He flukes the F.

'Good.'

Then he sees that there are notes to play with his left hand at the same time.

'I can't do it,' Taliesin says. He is ready to tell everything.

'Yes you can. Try it. C, F, and with the left . . .'

'I can't.'

There is a silence. A long gap.

'I know that you find the notes hard. We can go over them again if you like,' Billy says.

The pretence has to come to an end soon.

Another long and significant gap. Taliesin looks at the score and hangs his head.

'We don't have to continue if you don't want to. You can't force it,' Billy says. He coughs again and puts his hand to his mouth.

'My mother was hoping I'd be able to play her a carol by Christmas,' Taliesin says. 'I'm going to see her then.'

'It's you that matters,' Billy says. 'You've got to want to

do it for yourself first. It doesn't matter whether your mother or your father expect you to.'

Taliesin wants to say he'd like to keep trying. Instead he manages something nearer the truth. 'I like coming here for lessons.'

Billy seems happy at this.

'Well, that is a good reason to me. But your parents pay me to teach you. We'll have to crack these notes – go back to the beginning.'

Taliesin finds a focus, something to stare at hard to make the problem go away. On top of the piano he notices a photograph of a man wearing a rugby jersey and a curiously ill-fitting cap on his head. The childish cap is incongruous on this Grown-Up. The player has no neck and his smile reveals only three teeth. The photograph is signed.

'You'll have to start with the first book we used – John Thompson's book,' Billy says. 'I can't make you want to do it. You've got time on your side. I was forty when I started. My Skin Clock stayed up for over a second and a half.'

Taliesin finds his hand being taken up in Billy's warm encompassing hand. He is slightly conscious of his warts.

'Hold out your hand, like so,' Billy says. 'Then pinch the skin on the back of your hand. That's your Skin Clock.' Taliesin's skin twangs back. 'It's elastic, see. It's young skin. It shows you that it's early in your life. Plenty of time for piano; plenty of time for anything. Pinch mine, right there on the back on my hand, that's it. And look at it. It stays pinched for three seconds, at least. It sits up like that. It's late in my life. There are only so many things I can do now. You can do many things.' Billy's Skin Clock is slow and mottled, marked by age. Taliesin's Skin Clock is sprightly, twanging back to its original position with time on its side. 'The thing is not to have a fear for those notes,' Billy goes on. 'They're there to help you. I had exactly the same problem. I hated them. They always seemed superior, staring back from the page.'

'I've been pretending all this time,' Taliesin admits. With the admission he feels something lift off his chest.

'If you didn't have such a good ear, I'd have noticed it a long time ago. The thing is you've raced ahead, because you pick things up here and not here.' Billy points from Taliesin's ear to his head.

Taliesin asks Billy who the man in the photograph is.

'Spud Williams – plays for Wales,' Billy says.

'How do you know him then?'

'He's been here a couple of times.'

'For piano?'

'No. I was helping him with his shoulder – healing.'

'Is that what all these people come here for, like that lady?'

'Yes.'

Taliesin didn't expect Billy to say it straight out.

'What do you do?' he asks.

Billy holds out his hands. 'I lay these on people and pray for them to be healed. And sometimes, with God's help, they are.'

Taliesin tries to picture this, seeing only boiling pots and wands, a wizard's hat, and bubbling troubling cauldrons: all the clichés of magic he can conjure. He'd like to be an apprentice.

'Do you cast a spell?' he asks.

'It's a prayer. It's simple. You could do it. The hard part is believing you can do it. That's why we're not all doing it. Anyone can heal if they believe in the power of God,' Billy says. To hear God mentioned in this way is exciting and unnerving.

'What do I have to believe?' Taliesin asks, wanting to get it right.

'That there is a God. That you can ask him to heal.'

'Could I see you do it – to that lady?'

Billy puts his hands together.

'We'll have to ask Mrs Willis if she minds. People are funny.'

'I'd like to learn how to do it,' Taliesin says.

'We'll have to do some kind of deal. You learn the notes properly and I'll teach you how to heal.'

Taliesin holds out his hand and the two Skin Clocks meet in time – small and large, cool and warm. The sorcerer makes his pact with his apprentice.

A car pulls into the drive. Taliesin goes to the window and sees the lady bent like a tree in the wind being helped from the car by a young man holding out his elbow to steady her. She is so stooped that a simple push would send her tumbling head over heels. As she is led through to the sitting room, Billy introduces Taliesin as his pupil.

'Taliesin is going to help me pray for you today, Mrs Willis. I was going to start him off on a few cuts and scratches, just to see how he got on, but I think your back could do with an extra hand.' Mrs Willis doesn't seem to mind this. She is more concerned with herself.

'Oh God, Mr Evans, I can't describe the pain. The doctor can't do anything for me. He just keeps giving me aspirin. I'll give you anything if you could take the pain away. Do you think it'll be over with today, Mr Evans. What do you think? I can't tell you how much my back hurts. If I take any more painkillers . . . agh!' She stops and looks at Taliesin, having to move her whole body to look. 'Just you wait, young man, your turn will come. Ow, I do hope you can do something for me Mr Evans. I have to say I felt a little better after the first session but it's got worse this last few days. Jean told me you were a marvel. You should see her since she saw you – right as rain. I think it's amazing what you've done. I was ever so sceptical when she told me. Please don't take offence at that Mr Evans, but I never thought . . . anyway, I don't care what people say. If you can heal me Mr Evans I don't care how you do it. I am prepared to believe anything. I'm open-minded. Jean thinks you're a marvel. And you do it all for free. How long will it take, do you think?'

Mrs Willis is a chunterer; she seems to have a phobia for silences, even the necessary silences between words. From the moment she enters the house, escorted by her son (who says nothing), she is talking as if letting in the quiet might show there's something wrong with the world.

'I think we'll need a few more sessions yet, Mrs Willis. We'll have to see what God can do. Will you sit over here?'

'I think it's marvellous that you do it all for free. You should start charging people, Mr Evans, you'd make a fortune, although I suppose you don't want to do that, it wouldn't be right would it?'

'Right you are.'

Taliesin stands rather awkwardly in the corner of the room. Mrs Willis doesn't seem to mind him being there. She sits in the chair in front of the gas fire, her back curving forward from the chair, her old Skin Clocks gathering in loose layers on the backs of her hands, already raised with little time left to tick. Once she's in the chair her son excuses himself, saying that he'll wait in the car.

'Right now, just relax, Mrs Willis,' Billy orders.

'Yes, yes. It's not easy to relax with this back, Mr Evans.'

Taliesin watches Billy's hands spreading there on the old lady's spine. They are spread out wide as if warming at a fire.

'So how is Mrs Griffiths?' Billy asks, getting her to relax.

'Oh, you've done wonders for her Mr Evans. She's completely healed.'

'What are your first names again Mrs Willis?'

'Jane Megan.'

'Jane Megan. Jane Megan. Good. That's good. It helps me to know, see. When I'm praying it helps to know the names.'

'I hope you can do something for me Mr Evans. I need a miracle.'

With three people the room is even more cramped and airless and an unlikely place for a miracle. The healing is very matter of fact. There are no histrionic chants, no theatrical gestures. Billy runs his warm hands down the lady's back, following the buckled camber of the spine, praying to himself. His lips move slowly and Taliesin catches a Jesus here and there. The lady relaxes to his touch. After five minutes of quiet concentration Billy stops. He slips easily from intense prayer back to light chattering. He starts to talk about other healings and Taliesin is all ears.

'I had a boy here last week, twelve years old, same age as you, Taliesin. He couldn't even walk. His mother came with him and expected me to fix her boy up in one go. She was desperate. I tried my best. As I said, I never know when or why it works. You can never be sure when God is going to help and when He isn't. I just have to believe that He's going to help me every time.'

Billy motions to Taliesin. 'Put your hand here.'

Taliesin, hardly believing what he's doing, places his hand on the lady's shoulder, uncertain of how much pressure to apply. She is bony, brittle and cool.

'Ask God to heal Mrs Willis,' Billy says.

Taliesin expects to feel and see something – electric currents or lightning shooting from the end of his fingers. But all he feels and sees is the breathing of Mrs Willis who has her eyes closed, and the soft murmuring of Billy Evans, whispering pianissimo prayers. The lady seems to relax to his touch. It is an extraordinary thing to do and yet it feels utterly meant, as natural as drinking tea. He is healing someone, playing a duet alongside his teacher and all it requires is belief.

Billy smiles as he prays, assured of things hoped for, certain of things not seen. He runs his hand vertically down the back and then horizontally across the shoulders, drawing out a cross. Taliesin watches Billy's lips and tries to pray too. He repeats the prayer in his head over and over. 'Heal her back, please heal her back.' Every now and again he mimics Billy and adds the name of Jesus, a name that has the power to both embarrass and delight.

This is a magic of some kind. Right here in this stuffy bungalow there is a magic being unleashed and channelled unseen through the hands of his piano teacher and through his own hands too. It is a sweet music of possibility and it is playing here in his village; not in a jungle with drums drumming, O Dearly Beloved; not in a castle with pipes piping, nor leagues beneath the ocean with starfish dancing; but here in this very normal, very dull place that doesn't even feature in his atlas.

As they pray, Mrs Willis moves back her neck and starts to straighten up. She opens her mouth but for once can't find words. Taliesin watches the small, crumpled woman lose years as she extends her back and unbends.

'That's it, let it come,' Billy says.

Taliesin keeps his hands there on Mrs Willis's back, not really believing that he's helping much. Billy's the one who's doing it, he thinks. Mrs Willis's mouth is still open, emitting soundless words. Then Taliesin feels movement under his hand, a hard pressing movement.

'I can move it,' she says, in a whisper now. Taliesin can feel the movement. Mrs Willis sounds different now, so much quieter than before. She's stopped talking rubbish. 'You've done it, Mr Evans. Something's happened to me. I don't know what you've done, but you've done it,' she says.

Billy's lips are still moving. He appears to be thanking someone other than himself. Taliesin has forgotten to breathe and he feels sudden drumming inside his chest. Mrs Willis is crying. 'Thank you, Mr Evans. Thank you,' she says.

'It's not me, Mrs Willis,' Billy says. 'Don't thank me.'

CHAPTER SEVEN

AT NIGHT, the questions come: why am I here and not there? Why am I me and not them? Before I was me, where was I? Where will I be when I'm not me? Taliesin stares at the wall for answers.

The walls of his bedroom are covered in a vivid blue-flowered paper and the patterns have a mesmeric quality. There are four distinct motifs: a fleur-de-lys, a daffodil, a tulip, and a rose. Trying to find the beginnings and ends of these flowers is a kind of prayer. Lying in bed with the light on staring at the ceiling can be like space travel – the un-broken swirls of the patterns seeming as infinite as eternity itself.

He pushes his warmed feet into the cool patches and shuns *Just So Stories*. Taliesin now knows how the elephant got its trunk, how the leopard earned its spots and how the camel received its hump. They're all good reasons although none of them are mentioned in *The Encyclopedia of the Living World*. What he'd like to know now is How The Boy Got His Warts. He notices the two warts on the end of his index finger and a new third one on his middle finger that must have sprung on him in the dark.

Another fantastic story comes to mind. Since the extra-ordinary experience in Billy Evans's sitting room, Taliesin has relived that back-straightening feat a thousand times, trying to recall it as precisely as he can so that he might catch the very moment of the change. He sees Mrs Willis before the prayer and after, his hand hovering on her bony back. He remembers her tears as she was escorted to the car, the little jig she did in the yard and the astonishment of her son at the sight. And then Billy's calm matter of factness. How The Lady Had Her Back Straightened is a story that he'd like to tell.

He tries to pray. He experiments by putting his hands out as if receiving rain drops but he feels self-conscious and retracts them, drawing them together in a simple pyramid, with the tips of his warty fingers just below his lip and his thumbs pressing against his chest. This was the way he used to do it in primary school. This familiar symmetry seemed the right and only way to talk to God. He prayed then with his eyes shut tight, but he has now prayed with his eyes open and seen a response. From now on he intends to keep them open. Someone is listening to his prayers, listening with interest – someone who can make seventy-year-old backs straighten.

He tries to focus on what he thinks is God and waits for the words. But the words don't come. An indisciplined jumble of ungodly things appear, shopping lists of things he wants. God has always been an unseen certainty that he has trusted in, like the fact that India is hot even though he has never experienced its heat. Now that he tries to picture God he sees anything but God. He forces himself to imagine. He thinks about space going on and on. He's going on and on and out and out past stars and towards stars. He travels like this for five minutes until he comes to a wall – the end of space. But there must be something on the other side of the wall; even nothing is something, so he passes on to another infinity. He gives up trying to imagine God. He reverts to the picture in his *Illustrated Bible*: that hand coming through the cloud. And these hands become Billy's hands, and then they are Julie Dyer's hands holding Hooper's four fingers.

Uncomfortable images dance through his mind. Julie Dyer and his mother, almost indistinguishable and disconcertingly naked; Hooper joining them and pointing and laughing at Taliesin's father who sits bowed, ashamed of himself. Apple-grabbers, lawbreakers, troublemakers.

Lying on his side with his ear pressed into the pillow he can hear his heart beating and feel it too. He concentrates on that beat, the surest sign that he is alive and he finds it disconcerting. It should be reassuring like the sea in a shell or a mother's bosom, but it makes him uneasy. He tries to sleep but it's too early and his head is question-throbbed.

He turns over onto his right side where the beat is quieter and he starts to count sheep. For variety he imagines the sheep in different colours: red-blue; red and blue; red with green stripes; blue with orange polka dots. But the colours are too elusive to imagine and the sheep end up white. Perhaps if his father farmed elephants or camels things would be different. He tries counting camels, and then elephants.

He feels his breathing changing, sinking. He sinks, drifting at the edge and then the current sucks him under . . .

He is at West Haven in a red boat. He can see the harbour but there don't seem to be any people in the town. Perhaps he's too far away to see them. The boat is called *Christmas* and there is a man at the bow looking out to sea. He has long thick matted hair which needs cutting. He can't see the man's face because his back is to him. The sea is choppy, licking at the sides of the little boat; a fragile little boat. Eventually the boat begins to rock so much that water spills in and slowly fills it. As it fills it gets heavier and as it get heavier it sinks a little further and as it sinks more water gets in. The sky is banded with long sausage-shaped clouds and further out the sea is darker and agitated. Looking back to land the weather is brighter and calmer. He'd like to turn the boat back to the port only the man is steering with a locked steely arm, oblivious to the rising water level in the boat. He could dive in but it's too far to swim and there are shapes lurking in the deep. The water rises and suddenly the boat lurches and flounders, tilting backwards as the water pours in . . .

He wakes and instantly feels the shame of his own water turning cold and clammy against his skin and spreading in a patch underneath him. He hopes that he is still dreaming but that acrid ammonia smell doesn't lie, nor does the yellow stain in the middle of the bed. He pulls the pastel striped sheet off and kneads it into a ball. The smell creeps and seeps everywhere, trying to tell the world. He peels off his pyjama bottoms and slips on some underpants before tip-toeing out of the room with the soiled sheet.

On the landing Taliesin hears a voice; what sounds like a conversation going on. He moves down a couple of steps and peers through the banisters. His father is standing in the kitchen looking ahead, as if addressing somebody. He starts pacing up and down the flagstone floor in the kitchen, his arms gesticulating, reasoning with an imagined somebody who isn't seeing his side of the argument.

'You may be right about that . . . yes. After all, you know best. You're the practical one and I'm the one who's getting carried away. But you can see that it's a good idea, that it would work, can't you see that? Let me show you. It's not like America.' His father continues the charade with utmost conviction, moving to the table where the map is still spread. He places a finger at one end of the topography and draws an encompassing circle around the perimeter of the land. He seems to continue his odd soliloquy in his head, running his finger over the map. Then he looks for an answer in the face of the imagined person, somewhere in the wall. Taliesin recognizes the person who isn't there as his mother, no doubt shaking her head and raising her eyebrows at this latest offering. There is something tender in the way his father looks at the wall, as if he's really seeing her there.

Taliesin is caught between not wanting to embarrass his

66

father by interrupting him, and embarrassing himself by being seen with his liable bundle. He opts to put the sheet into the basket and leave his father with his wall.

The next morning Taliesin finds his father hauling a trunk into the hallway. He looks rough with his stubble becoming beard.

'What are you doing, Da?'

'Your mother wants the rest of her stuff.' In the last few days there has been a spate of long, argumentative phone calls between his father and mother. They have invariably ended with a slammed phone and a curse.

In the trunk there are nightgowns, undergarments, brassieres, shoes, a dressing gown, dresses, skirts, a hat with a maroon bandana, the silk scarf that hung on the end peg, the silver-back brush and matching mirror, a washbag filled with make-up, a velvet bag with a necklace, a mahogany writing box, a picture of the sea that hung over his parents' bed, records, and books – all jumbled pell-mell in the trunk like priceless treasures.

'This was a wedding present from my mother – your grandmother. If anyone should have this, you should,' his father says, holding up the writing box. It is a beautiful thing, probably a priceless thing. Taliesin once wrote a thank you letter on it to his aunt thanking her for his *Illustrated Bible* and a bobble hat that he never wore.

'She's certainly changed her tune,' his father continues. 'She wants half the furniture too. She's bloody welcome to it, but she's not having this. I want you to have the box, here, take it.'

Taliesin takes the box from him. His father is showing a new anger now that he is waking up to the fact that his wife isn't coming back. He could be a shepherd or a wise man with that beard but Taliesin knows that it takes more than age, a flowing cape and a camel to make someone wise. It wasn't that long ago that Taliesin thought his father knew everything there was to know in life. He had all the answers to things: the tallest mountain in Wales, the longest river, the population of Peking. He knew how to deliver a lamb and fix a tractor engine. He knew lots of things. But his status as the cleverest, wisest and strongest man has taken a dent. There are things his father doesn't know. He isn't always sure. He has weaknesses. And now he talks to walls.

'Before I send this lot off why don't you see what you want for yourself. There's books in here.' Taliesin has seen them, the gold, bold love books with curling script on the covers. 'And there's records. Jon will want some of these things. Maybe you should have this too.' His father hands Taliesin a photograph album with an ivory cushioned cover, a date and his parents' initials engraved in everlasting gold.

'I'm going to get some more stuff from the loft; maybe you could fetch the rest of your mother's clothes from the chest of drawers.' He rises stiffly, scowling, begrudging the time he's using up. He brushes his hands as if he's just performed the filthiest task of his life.

Taliesin has seen the wedding album once before. The pictures have lost none of their fascination. Each photograph covers the entire page; a thin sheet of tracing paper protecting the photograph from dust and time. The first picture shows his mother arriving at the church with her father. She is slightly plumper than she is now and her smile belongs to a far distant time. Taliesin's grandfather's suit is entirely without crease or rumple and his white collar is whiter than his daughter's wedding gown. He looks as though he could be a wise man, even without the beard. There are a series of photographs of friends and family some of whom Taliesin recognizes. Everyone is smiling, filled with a hope and genuine expectation that seems ingenuous now. Those smiles seem say-cheese smiles, put on for the camera. The picture of his father is striking. He is so young, almost too young; and cocky like Jonathan, with a clean youthful chin that doesn't yet need a daily shave. There are more photographs taken in front of the chapel door, in different combinations: his parents on their own, looking a little lost but still smiling; his parents with their parents, bridesmaids, bestman; everyone wearing a stilted happiness, the kind of happiness that couldn't last. The album ends with his parents looking back over their shoulders through the rear window of a sedan, setting off on their lives together. It's a picture book, a fairy tale that must have been believable once. Taliesin closes the book, puts it back in the trunk and goes up to collect the rest of his mother's things.

His parents' bedroom is just his father's room now, but his mother's presence is there in the colour of the bedspread, the curtains and the wallpaper. She still somehow owns this room. The dressing table, even without the hairbrush and matching silver-backed hand mirror, should have her grooming in front of it. The top drawers of the chest still contain some of his mother's underwear. He throws the lingerie onto the bed.

The double bed is badly made, the sheet hanging lower than the counterpane. His father's side of the bed is indicated by his blue nylon pyjamas on top of the pillow. His slippers are on the floor and there is a newspaper and a farming magazine open at an article about property value.

His mother's side of the bed is unruffled and Taliesin wonders if at night his father spreads out his legs into the cool patches of bed where his mother used to sleep. Taliesin carries the remainder of his mother's lingerie downstairs and finds his father emptying more drawers. It seems that his mother has hoarded things away in strange places.

Taliesin holds out the intimate bundle. His father takes the lingerie picking out a white brassiere which he holds up and examines for a moment as though recalling something.

'How many people did you have at your wedding?' Taliesin asks.

'Too many. We didn't have enough drink for everyone.'

'How old were you when you got married?'

'Too young. Twenty-three.'

At twenty-three you couldn't be a wise man.

The telephone rings.

'Will you get that? It'll be your mother. She'll want to know about the trunk.'

Taliesin picks up the phone and it's his mother.

'Taliesin is that you?' His mother's voice is obscure through a telephone and she sounds further away than West Haven. She could be in Bombay or Brazil.

'Hi Mum.'

He pictures her in the off-white satin of the fairy album, smiling like there's no tomorrow.

'Darling, I'm glad you've answered. Are you well?' She sounds nervous, a little jabbery.

'Yeah, I'm fine.'

'Has your father rung the station about the trunk, do you know?' He notices how she says 'your father.' It's all part of her disassociation.

'I don't know. Do you want me to ask him?'

'No, no, don't worry. How are you?'

'I'm fine, Mum.'

'How's Jon?'

'He's fine. He's working down the farm.'

'How is school?'

'Fine.'

'And are you practising?'

'Yeah.' He lies.

'Toni says hello. He says he's looking forward to meeting you at Christmas. And Leo says hello.'

'Say hello back.'

'Tal says hello back, Leo. Well look Darling, tell your

father that I can pick up the trunk tomorrow. There are some fish knives. They're in the top drawer of the sideboard in the sitting room. We can leave the furniture 'til Easter or something. I'm going to leave you the piano. Tell your father that he doesn't need to send the trunk until tomorrow.'

'Okay.'

'And give my love to Jonathan. Has he decided what to do about Christmas?'

'I'm not sure,' he lies again.

'Well, try and persuade him to come. How is your father? Is he all right?'

'He's okay,' Taliesin says.

'And lots of love to you, Darling.'

'Okay.'

'Love you.'

'Yeah.'

'Bye.'

'Bye.'

'Oh, just one more thing: the carriage clock. Don't forget to wrap it. All right now. Bye.'

'Bye.'

The fish knives and forks are exactly where his mother said they would be. They lie in a velvet inlaid box. The forks have hallmarks and a shell motif at their ends, the knives have bone handles. There are enough for six place settings. She always talked about wanting four children.

'Bung these curtains in the chest if you can,' his father says, dumping the yellow velvet onto the floor. 'What did she want?'

'She said she can pick up the trunk tomorrow. And she wanted these fish knives.'

His father takes the knives and forks.

'Never knew we had these. We'll have nothing left at this rate. She'll want the television next. Put these in then.'

Taliesin folds the curtains and squeezes them into the box.

71

He fetches the stopped clock from the mantlepiece, still un-wound since she left. By getting rid of this clock they may move on from this limbo state, he thinks. He wraps it in newspaper and finds space for it between underwear and cutlery. The box is now crammed, like a treasure chest bound for a far distant seaport, filled with the bounty of a once happy marriage.

CHAPTER EIGHT

JUST-DROPPED LEAVES carpet the path to the gorge. The wood is just past golden, the trees growing skeletal, showing themselves. Taliesin takes two strides to his father's one and their coats make noises as the arms brush against their bodies. Some of the leaves seem to be hanging on for their lives, waiting for a small breeze to end it all. There is a crisp wind up now and it whispers to the leaves to drop and they say, 'No, not just yet, let us stay here golden for a few more days, then at least you can make a noise rustling through us; after all without us you are silent; we are your instruments.' This way they bargain with their lives.

Taliesin's father wants to convince his son that his latest plan can work. He has made some connection between this plan working and his wife coming back because of it.

'I'm going to show you something,' his father says.

The cave was once a place where Taliesin played a game called Run From The Dragon. It was an uncomplicated game that involved running from the cave to the top end of the wood without looking over your shoulder. The point of the race wasn't to come first, it was all about making the other person look back. If you looked back then you lost the game. It was hard for a young boy with a lively imagination not to believe there was something there when his older brother said there was. For Jonathan it was always a simple victory. Jonathan's literal competitive mind kept his gaze fixed firmly ahead. It was easy for him to win the game. There were times when Taliesin was convinced that he could smell the beast and feel its heat licking at his neck. His fear conjured images of a magnificent monster: twenty foot wingspan, crimson scales and amethyst eyes. Jonathan's ceaseless commentary augmented this picture. 'It's right behind us, it's almost got us. Don't look behind, whatever you do, don't look behind.'

The dragon was their father's fictitious creation – the supposed last dragon in Wales, inhabitant of the cave. He encouraged his sons to believe fervently in its existence, fuelling their belief with bedtime stories featuring the heroic brothers Tal and Jon. But when, during a particularly convincing run, Taliesin fell and chipped his tooth, his mother suggested that it was time to give up these silly games before someone got seriously hurt.

He can hear his mother now, telling him to give up his childish fantasies, while his father tries to encourage him. His mother's voice is sensible; his father's voice half-jesting. His mother gets crosser. His father laughs at her seriousness. And on they argue their universal argument, his father enjoying being a devil's advocate, his mother getting more impatient.

A line of beech trees borders the end of the field as if guarding a secret. The wind has got to their leaves and almost stripped them. The trees form an arboreal wall behind which the land drops down into the gorge flush with ferns, scree and dead wood now turned gold. Large boulders lie around as if randomly thrown by an irate giant. The entrance to the cave is conspicuous but awkward to get to. At a cursory glance the opening looks no more than a minor recess, but with enough light and curiosity any explorer could see that there's something there. They climb the ledge and his father stretches out his hand and pulls him up.

'We'll need to make some steps here,' he says.

He shines the torch ahead and the beam creates dancing shadows against the green-tinged rock. A horizontal passage lies ahead, clear and eerily virgin. Taliesin's father has to crouch like an ape to enter and it narrows and cools with every step taken into it. Soon the beam picks out patches of water and dripping calcium. Then the tunnel widens and on either side small stalactites appear gripping to the ceiling and dripping to the floor where stalagmites grow up to meet them in another millenium. An ivory skeletal forest fills the cavern, dripping with time. The rocks must be Cambrian, his atlas of the world showed most of Wales as a purple Cambrian. He tries to recall the rest of the names: Pre-Cambrian; Cambrian; Ordovician; Silurian; Devonian; Carboniferous and Permian.

'I think people will pay to see this,' his father says.

'I'm freezing,' Taliesin says.

'We'll have to put a heater in here. Just here by the entrance.'

Unconsciously their voices have dropped to a whisper as if in a chapel or a church. Even their whispers amplify and shimmer with echo.

'Hello,' his father calls. 'Hello, hello, hello.' The word bounces and chases itself around the cave. They wait for the silence to return. Taliesin knows that there isn't anything here. Not a sound comes from the cave; no reply to the call. Not so long ago he would have expected a booming roar or spouting flame to drive them away but now he hears only silence and drips. He was running from nothing but his imagination. The dragon is retreating fast in his mind, running from the inevitable appearance of maturity and sense. He can't recall that cruel symmetry with the same clarity. The head-ripping red has faded, the jagged, air-slicing wings are limp, his flame is a damp squib, unable to singe the knight's charger, and the tail spiralling devilishly to a harsh tip is flaccid and broken.

The dragon is now an idea that has atrophied. It's just an idea sitting in that deep, wet cavern breathing slower than a grandfather, listening to the drips and to the whispered rumours of its extinction, unable to muster more than a faint

75

moan which people mistake for the wind. Taliesin knows now that he doesn't have to run any more and that if he turned around there would be no amethyst eyes beading down on him.

'Listen,' his father says. But Taliesin can only hear their breathing. He has almost two breaths to his father's one, the same as the footsteps. 'Well, what do you think?' his father asks. In truth it is cold and damp and Taliesin would rather be somewhere else. The magic of the cave is something that exists in his father's head, not his. The stories which once meant so much and were so convincing, no longer hold sway over him. He doesn't even feel fear at being in this place, the very front room of the dragon's lair. As he looks into the blackness he knows that there is nothing there but the fancy that his mother saw.

CHAPTER NINE

HOW HOOPER LOST HIS FINGER is the subject of Class Assembly. Hooper starts as if everyone is against him and then, seeing the class respond well to his more outrageous claims, he begins to enjoy himself, taking liberties with the truth. Taliesin finds the tale unamusing. For him, it doesn't work. What starts as a plausible retelling soon deteriorates into something unbelievable. Hooper is concerned with impressing the class with quantity rather than quality. He pumps hyperbole into the tale. The tractor is The Heaviest Tractor in Wales. His finger was trapped in the cutter and there was enough blood to fill a swimming pool. Plus, he had to lever The Heaviest Tractor in Wales off his hand. (Cries of 'You never'. Replies of 'I bloody did'.)

Hooper is at his most excessive when talking about pain and blood. The class seem to love it, laughing louder as the facts become more fabulous. Hooper responds like a genie who can double any statistic and multiply it by ten. His story has an organic quality. It seems to grow and grow: ten becomes twenty, hours become days, a cottage hospital becomes The Biggest Hospital in Wales and then the world in only one sentence.

As Hooper receives the applause, Taliesin wonders how the class would react to the story of Mrs Willis. One or two might be interested, but even Julie Dyer seems taken in by Hooper's swank. Despite her claims of hatred towards Hooper, he can see her laughing. This is hard to account for. What she says isn't what she does.

Besides, what's a back being straightened compared to these magnificent fibs? They'd find it too mysterious and bloodless. Sure, they might believe that he prayed for an old woman; they might accept that he laid his hands on her back to do this; but they would never believe that the lady arrived doubled up and left standing as straight as a skyscraper. 'Don't throw your pearls to pigs,' Billy told him. Taliesin remembers this advice and seeing the snorting class around him he decides that now isn't the time to share these things.

This day has the first presage of winter in it, an extra bite that makes Taliesin's nipples stand up. He is in the school yard with Luc Daniel, playing jacks. The ground is wet so they squat on their haunches and their mouths shoot out vapours like spirits. Taliesin is wearing gloves which serve the double purpose of keeping the cold from his hands and his warts from the world. He has eleven warts now, clustering around his fingertips – four on his left hand, seven on his right. The original wart has spawned a callous offspring that can no longer be hidden by clenching his hand. They are conspicuous enough for other people to notice them and make comment. Every time Luc Daniel passes up the jacks he rubs his hands off.

'I won't catch any germs from you through the gloves, will I?' he asks.

'Probably not,' Taliesin says.

'How do you get warts, anyway?' Luc asks.

'I don't know,' Taliesin replies, although he's had plenty of conflicting advice. His father has told him to keep washing his hands and not shake hands with anyone he likes; his brother said that's what you get for reading too many books and turning too many dirty, yellowed pages. The grocer talked about the need for more vitamins, recommending apples, kiwis and parsley – which has the highest content of vitamin C of any known food, apparently. Beyond apples, curbing his

78

reading habits and time, no other cure has been suggested.

Taliesin is convinced that they are a sign of some kind, a sign from God. But as divine communication goes these crusty lumps are hardly sublime. Perhaps they are a punishment for something that he has done – asking too many questions, telling lies, wetting his bed. Or they might be a reaction to his mother leaving home. Maybe his skin is hardening in response to events and becoming a kind of protective outer layer. There is a reason.

'My mum's going to do a fan-bloody-tastic recipe for you when you come round,' Luc enthuses. 'I told her that you didn't eat properly because you haven't got a mother around. I told her about your warts. She says you need a square meal.' Taliesin is glad of the invite but upset that his warts have to be the premise. He hasn't met Luc's mother before and now he won't be able to shake her hand. He pictures her talking to Luc and Luc holding out his hands for inspection, all clean. 'I told her all about you,' Luc continues. 'I told her how you like to read books all the time. I told her that you believe in God.'

Taliesin would like to tell Luc all about Mrs Willis and her amazing straightening back but he can't quite trust him. Luc might still prove a pig with his pearls. Although he is his best friend this has more to do with sitting next to each other during registration and a child's lack of prejudice than anything else. It is just one of those circumstantial friendships that could develop or not. They are not yet friends who would die for each other. Luc would never lay down his life for Taliesin, and Taliesin would find it hard to sacrifice his interesting life for Luc's. If they were washed up on an island – like those boys in that book he's reading now – Luc would be the first to daub himself in war paint; and if there was only enough food on the island for one he wouldn't flinch as he slipped a bamboo spear into his sleeping friend's heart. If Taliesin has a best friend it is still his books. He prefers the companionship of a good book. He could die for a good book, or a character in one. He could even die for characters in bad books. He would rather spend time with Ralph and Piggy or Snowball and Boxer.

It's not like the girls in his class. Boys don't have the same ability as girls to forge these meaningful best-friendships; they don't seem to share the same secrets and intimate details. Taliesin likes Luc but he never really listens to what he says. For a start, he has a distracting shaped mouth that does odd things when he talks and Taliesin has grown accustomed to Luc's once impressive splitting up of words and insertion of a word like 'bloody' in its middle. Taliesin admires Luc's enthusiasm for almost anything that moves but he's frustrated by his tendency to get bored quickly – the result of having parents that spoil him. (Already Luc is bored with his water-resistant to twenty-five metres watch with the chronograph dial that tells the time in India and Brazil simultaneously.)

And yet, for all this, Taliesin has a desire to share what he saw with his friend. He feels that it is treasure too valuable to bury.

'Are you all right?' Luc asks.

'What?'

'Who were you talking to just then, when your lips were moving? You looked like you were talking to someone.'

'I was just thinking.'

'My father says that people who talk to themselves are a bit in the head. Men-bloody-tal. Ha!'

Taliesin thinks of his father's recent dialogue with the kitchen wall and wonders if it counts as talking to yourself if you really imagine you're talking to someone else.

He is close to telling Luc about Mrs Willis but the moment is lost as three boys stride towards them with arms interlocked chanting, 'Join on, join on for Bulldogs! Join on, join on for Bulldogs!' The three-headed game-caller stops in front of them, the cold air roaring from their linked Hydra heads. The middle head hisses first.

'Come on then Worm, join on.'

'No thanks,' he says.

One of the heads sees the early gloves.

'It's not even cold yet, Worm. Why you wearin' gloves?'

'I am cold,' he says and he moves his shoulders in a mock shiver to prove it.

'He's got warts,' Luc The Loyal says.

'Urgh. Don't you ever wash? Didn't your mother tell you about washing your hands Wormy warty, wormy, wiggly, warty worm?' the Hydra says.

Oddly Taliesin isn't stung by any of these taunts or even his best friend's perfidy. He knows how evil boys can be from the book he's reading. And anyway, he seems to have created a store for the insults; a kind of reservoir or a cesspool where he can sluice the detritus. Maybe the collective hurts will overflow some day, flooding his pool and bursting his banks. He's not cried in a long time, not since he was wrongly accused of stealing a book from his last school. And he didn't cry when his mother left home. He is developing a hard outer shell.

'Come on Luc,' the left head says.

Luc looks at Taliesin.

'I don't mind,' Taliesin says.

Luc Daniel wouldn't die for him so he won't tell him yet. The three-headed monster sprouts another head and strides on chanting, looking for more bulldogs.

On the bus home Julie Dyer smokes three cigarettes and paints her nails. She offers to paint Taliesin's nails but he keeps the gloves on thank you very much. She keeps ogling him covetously, as if he's an unopened Christmas present and she's about to rip off his thin wrapping and get to what is inside. Julie Dyer is changing shape and size more quickly than should be humanly possible. In a few months she has gone from being the girl with the almost-breasts to the girl with the quite-definitely-breasts. As a result reading has become very difficult. When the back end of the bus careers Taliesin finds himself deliberately letting his chicken legs press up against her elephantine thighs. She doesn't mind. They have become friends because of books, but his enthusiasm for reading on the bus has diminished in inverse proportion to her ballooning. Since *Animal Farm* she has become voracious for more readings, demanding two or three whole chapters at a go. She has this irritating habit of predicting what is going to happen, invariably getting it right.

'C'mon then, let's have *Lord Of The Flies*. What's going to happen to Piggy?' she asks. 'I want to know what they're going to do to him. They're going to kill him, I know that's what they're going to do. They're evil, those boys.'

He starts to read, the gloves making it hard to turn pages. Some of the language is obtuse and the action vague but it doesn't seem to matter; it communicates a sense. There is something terrible going to happen, Julie Dyer is right. Today, in the playground he saw the truth in this book; the truth that boys can be worse than animals. If he was on that island he'd be like Ralph. He'd try and remember the right way to lead his life, he wouldn't pick up a spear. Boys don't have to be bad. One day, he vows, he will form a gang and it will be good.

They reach the part where the boys gather on the beach, surrounding Piggy. The terrible thing is about to happen. He reads on. It is happening. He is reading the words, Piggy is falling. And yet he can't picture it. All he can feel is his leg and the heat of Julie Dyer's and his gloved hands trembling slightly as the book reaches its climax.

'Why don't you take the gloves off?' Julie inevitably asks.

'I get cold easily,' he says. This is weak given the suffocating heat at the back of the bus. She places a hand on his skinny knee.

'Come on, let me see. You're hiding something.'

Taliesin feels very warm. Julie has his hands in hers and she's peeling off the gloves.

'Urgh! Warts. Look at them all.'

Taliesin is sick with shame. He snatches back the gloves and pulls them on, unable to look at his hands. Julie is looking at her own hands and checking her manicured talons for signs of infection.

'You mustn't touch me,' she says. But she needn't fear for Taliesin is already making his way to the front of the bus.

The sky is the colour of blackcurrant jam. Taliesin has one thing on his mind now. These warts are more than an unwelcome distraction, taking up his thoughts, making it hard to read books and play the piano. They are in danger of making him an outcast. If he could cut off his hands now to stop them spreading to the rest of his body, he would. He's tried plasters but they made it worse, only incubating them. He can't help but feel guilty about them, a sense of shame that his gloves can't cover. His father's prediction that warts can take months to go is not what he wants to hear. He is impatient. Time may be the great healer but time doesn't have to suffer the consequences, it just carries on ticking oblivious. Swift medicine is what he wants; the immediate miraculous remedy. He needs someone who has the power to transcend time's natural laws; someone who can speed up the process. He needs Billy Evans – he does warts; they'll be nothing to him. Just a session, maybe two, that's all it'll take. It will be a cinch for someone who's done twisted spines. His touch can do it. Evans has the touch. Warts aren't even a disease. They're on the same level as a common cold. Billy won't be expecting him now, but that won't matter. He will go to him in faith and Billy will fix the warts with a cross and a prayer.

The blackcurrant sky is giving way to a clear blue darkness; the clouds that threatened have moved on, leaving Cwmglum dry. The shop where he buys his apples, the pub where his father drinks and the houses that are ugly all stand out in silhouette. Further up Straight Street the chapel floats like a small grey ark in a sea of gravestones. He's not been to chapel since he was too small to remember his parents taking him when they believed. That was years ago and the memory is one of old ladies with blue hair and hats; his mother's voice soaring high above the others to the point of embarrassment; his father going through the motions and using Taliesin as a diversion from the vague goings-on at the front; and a younger, sweeter Jonathan wearing a worsted wool coat that Taliesin inherited. Jonathan was a pious ten-year-old then; an earnest angel who looked as though he believed in what he was doing. Perhaps it was another phase of his, like swearing or rugby.

There is a car outside Billy's place and the lights are all on in the house. Taliesin has to knock several times before Billy comes to the door.

'Come in, come in. I've got someone with me,' he says.

Despite the unexpected timing of the call, Billy is full of grace and genuinely pleased to see him. Taliesin follows him into the gassy warmth. It has reached that stage of the year when it's preferable to be indoors.

'Tell me, are we meant to be having a lesson today?' Billy asks gently. 'Have I forgotten?'

'No. I wanted to see you about something,' Taliesin says.

'Fine. As long as I haven't forgotten a lesson or something. I'm getting forgetful.' Taliesin can hear people in the lounge.

'You'd better wait here while I fix up this man,' Billy whispers. 'I'd ask you to lend a hand but they're a bit funny. There's tea in the pot.'

Taliesin goes to the kitchen but the voices from the other room draw him to the door and he watches through the gap there. He can see the piano but that's unimportant now.

A young man of about twenty sits in the chair, naked from the waist up. Billy has one of his hands on the man's back and the other on his forehead. Another man, much older, and possibly the younger man's father, fidgets and looks around the room wanting to leave. Next to him a woman watches with concern. She must be the young man's mother judging from the way she takes the man's hand, sharing his discomfort. Her husband is aloof and uneasy with what is taking place before him. Billy performs the same routine that he did with Mrs Willis, even pausing half way through to tell of his latest successes and failures. Seen a second time the healing is more natural.

'I think this may take another two or three sessions,' Billy says. 'There's no telling how long it will take. That part is up to God.' The woman nods her head but her husband looks even more uneasy. After the healing he stands up, barely able to wait a minute longer.

'Is that it then?' he asks brusquely.

'For today, yes. Although you can do your bit and pray, Mr Thomas,' Billy winks at the man. The lady gives a firm assurance that they will pray.

'That's your job, Mr Evans. Isn't that what we're paying you for?' Mr Thomas says. He reaches into his pocket. 'How much do we owe you?'

'You don't owe me anything,' Billy says, without any hint of offending or being offended.

'Here. Take this,' the man says, holding out a note.

'That's kind, Mr Thomas, but I can't accept money. Thank you though.'

Even so, the man puts the money on the coffee table and weighs it down with a brass bell that tinkles as he places it there.

'Take it,' the man says and he walks away not wishing to discuss it further.

Billy asks the young man how he is feeling.

'I definitely felt something. I feel that I've got more energy.' He is pale and obviously too hollow in the cheek and his eyes are bloodshot. 'Do you think I'll be all right?' he asks.

'You'll need to come again. A couple of times. And if you want to pray too, you can. I tell everyone who comes here that they can do it. You can get your Mam and Dad to lay hands on you and pray.' Billy twinkles when he says this. Mr Thomas makes a sharp intake of breath.

'Thank you, Mr Evans. We must be off,' he says. Taliesin draws back from the door and washes up his cup while Billy shows the family to the door. He comes back shaking his head in dismay.

'I think his father thought I was some kind of wizard.' He walks slowly and coughs again. 'So how is my apprentice? Have you done any praying?'

Taliesin has tried and struggled. His words, he felt, were shot out into an empty, unheard void and echoed back to him unheeded. 'It was hard,' he says.

'I know it's difficult to pray. There are times when I shake my head and see only air. You have to trust; you have to step into it with your eyes open. It takes practice – like piano. The more you do it the sweeter the sound. Don't force it, it's natural, we've just forgotten how, that's all. Just talk as you would to a friend. You don't have to thee and thou your way to Him. Pray when you want to. It might be a Monday, first thing in the morning cleaning your teeth. Ask Him to bless your food, the weather, your family. There's nothing He doesn't know, so tell Him what's troubling you.'

'I tried to pray in bed the other night but I couldn't concentrate. I can't see Him. What does He look like?'

Billy gives a dry chuckle that makes his shoulders hunch and jig. 'That would be something, if you could picture God in your head. Some head. You get glimpses, mind. In thunder. In light. I see Him in the faces of people looking for something. They are really looking for Him. And He comes to me in the healing. That's when I see Him clearly.'

Billy starts to pack a pipe. He lights it and puffs and the smoke gathers cumulously around him. He becomes a medicine man conjuring the spirits of the air. The ethered fog sculpts weird images: a bull with wings, a bird without, something abstract and amorphous, a face – the face of a man with a beard. A sudden hollow dry cough makes him withdraw the pipe and clutch his ribs.

Taliesin looks down at his gloved hands and pulls a loose strand of wool.

'What have you got there?' Billy asks, still coughing.

Taliesin peels the gloves off and holds out his hands. Without hesitation Billy takes the infected hands in his. Taliesin feels ashamed at setting such a lowly problem before a healer who straightens backs and lifts the dark from blind eyes.

'Maybe I should just wait for them to go anyway, they're not very important,' he says.

'Everyone's complaint is worse than the next man's. Warts are warts. God is a mover of warts and mountains alike.' Now that Billy is prepared to pray for them the warts appear to grow and become all the more immovable. 'Anyway, these will need to be fixed before you put your fingers on my piano. If I get warts I won't be able to touch anyone. I'd be out of a job.' Billy smiles his irreverent smile that always surprises. 'Do you want them to be healed?'

Taliesin nods.

'Do you have a second name?'

'No.' His father always said that Taliesin was enough on its own.

'It's good to know the person's name, see,' Billy says. 'There is power in a name.' Billy takes Taliesin's hands at the wrists and closes his eyes. Taliesin keeps his eyes open and focused right there on his hands, watching his warts, half expecting them to spontaneously remit or shrivel up under the power. Does he feel something – a tingle, a buzz? Is there a supernatural heat flowing, or is that the pulsing of Billy's heat-generating hands?

'You're tensing up, relax.' Taliesin tries to relax. He follows Billy's lips now, trying to catch an abracadabra or a hocus-pocus. Again the only thing he hears is a 'Jesus.' When all is done Taliesin continues to stare at his hands waiting for something to happen.

'Why do you ask Jesus to heal them?'

'He showed us how to do these things,' Billy says. 'It's He who gives us the power to do it.'

'When will they go?' Taliesin asks, disappointed that they haven't gone in an instant.

'A couple of days should do it.'

'Is one session enough?'

'We'll see.'

The warts are still there – an unmoved, ugly sight. God's got his work cut out fixing them and it will be a miracle if He does.

Billy takes Taliesin's hand in his.

'Remember what I said to you last week. You can do it too. With enough faith you can do what I do. I told these people that today and they looked at me as though I was joking. I am not joking, you must realize this. People come to me and they look at me as if I'm special; they think it's all down to me. That's what happens when they don't believe in God. They make idols of people. If they could see that it was God they wouldn't treat me the way they do – like a magician, like an entertainer. But this isn't entertainment, it's real life and death.'

Billy doesn't try to promote a mystique but even as he speaks these demystifying words, Taliesin can't but feel that Billy is special, that he does have something that other people don't have. The spiritual accessibility of which he speaks still seems fantastically out of reach; beyond the powers of an eleven-year-old boy who can't imagine God and doesn't know how to pray. Surely he will have to be a wise man of at least fifty before he can do the things that Billy Evans does?

CHAPTER TEN

LUC THE SHIRT'S house is modern and clean which is a
surprise – Taliesin thought the house would be dishevelled.
As they arrive in the late afternoon they enter the house to the
drone of a vacuum cleaner. A woman in trousers is hoover-
ing the hallway carpet as if she's in a competition. She is so
absorbed and the whine of the hoover so loud that she fails to
notice the boys' entrance.

'Hi Mum,' Luc says and he drifts past her with the non-
chalance that comes of having a mother around all the time.
His shirt is hanging out as much as it possibly can in protest at
his mother's unstoppable tidiness. Mrs Daniel has long curly
auburn hair and nails that are painted the colour of blood, the
same as Julie Dyer. She is tall for a woman, tall even for a
short man. And she is cleaner than a carpet. Mrs Daniel looks
up and sees him. She switches off the machine and it drones
down.

'Hello,' she says.

'Hello.'

'Luc? Aren't you going to introduce me to your friend?'

Luc shouts from the other room, 'This is Tal – careful not
to shake his hands.'

'I hope you've taken your shoes off, Luc.'

Taliesin smells a cocktail of nail varnish, perfume and hot
Hoover. Luc Daniel is lucky to have these smells in his house.

'We've heard a lot about you,' she says.

Taliesin dreads to think: warts, believing in God, malnutri-
tion, separated parents. None of it attractive information.

She sees his gloves and though she says nothing Taliesin knows that she knows.

'Is it Taliesin or do you prefer Tal?'

'I don't mind,' he says, just being polite. Actually he prefers Tal. Taliesin is too formal and is used to admonish, to remind him of exactly who he is. His mother would enunciate the name as if to say this is your name and I gave it to you. She would say the first three syllables of his name quickly and raise her voice on the final 'Sin'.

'It's an unusual name, even in Wales. I don't think I've met another Taliesin anywhere,' Mrs Daniel says. Her beauty is a transfixing thing and she has an English accent. 'Come in and have some tea and biscuits,' she says.

In the sitting room Taliesin scrutinizes his surroundings with a begrudging eye, comparing things to his own home. The Daniels' television is bigger but they haven't got a real fire; the house is clean but there aren't any books anywhere; the kitchen is part of the dining room and there isn't much of a garden. But they have more clocks and someone who winds them. There are clocks everywhere. Two clocks on the mantlepiece, a grandmother clock in the corner and a station clock above the dining room table. The house is filled with the sound of ticking; some like the hard tapping of woodpeckers, others like the slow beating of old hearts. They all tell the same quarter-to-six-o'clock time.

'Hey, look at this,' Luc says.

A mouse is killing a cat. Taliesin watches and they start to laugh as the cat walks into a rake and its head becomes rake shaped. More cats appear, doing human things. One of the clocks chimes once to indicate the quarter hour. Taliesin finds the clocks more interesting than the television.

'I've got a cuckoo clock in my bedroom, do you want to see it?' Luc asks.

'Yeah, okay.'

Taliesin is curious and still comparing things, trying to

establish some sort of superiority in his mind. The rest of the house is even cleaner than downstairs. At the top of the stairs there are towels and linen, washed and folded, plump with luxury. Luc's bedroom is bigger than Taliesin's but then his friend is an only child so he gets to choose. The room is cluttered with parental over-indulgences: too many toys, everything the latest and greatest. These toys account for Luc's low boredom threshold. He has too many and the way they're arranged around the room shows that he's bored with all of them. It looks as though he's tried them all once and then discarded them. Only the cuckoo clock seems to have retained its novelty for him.

'My Dad got it for me on a business trip. He got it from Switzerland. It'll come out soon, at six.'

Taliesin remembers that Switzerland is a place where apples are important. In Switzerland, William Tell balanced an apple on his son's head and shot an arrow at it; that's how confident he was. He was prepared to kill his own son to show how good he was. That was some faith.

They sit and wait for the clock to strike six, listening to the hollow ticking of the picture-book clock with its Swiss chalet design. At six a cuckoo comes out and hoots the hours. Downstairs all the clocks in the sitting room chime in unison, telling the world that things are still moving on. At the foot of the bed Taliesin sees a plastic gun that fires rubber sucker arrows.

'I know a good game,' he says. 'We need an apple.'

'I'll get one,' Luc says. He returns with a Golden Delicious. Taliesin hands him the gun and takes the apple, putting it on his head. He stands at the other end of the bedroom in the corner, the apple precariously perched on his skull. His posture is practised and the apple sits there.

'Try and shoot it off,' Taliesin says. 'You mustn't hit me though.'

'Easy,' Luc says, loading the arrow. He fires and it flies

past Taliesin's left eye and clatters into the wardrobe. The second hits him in the shoulder. Taliesin steadies the apple and tells Luc to imagine that these arrows are real and that he can't hit any part of the body that might kill.

'Just imagine that I am your son and that one shot will kill me,' he says.

The third arrow just misses the apple, lifting some of Taliesin's hair with a rush. Taliesin tries to look straight at the sucker head of the arrow and not close his eyes. He knows it's a harmless cartoon arrow but he tries to see it as a steel-tipped ebony shaft.

'Yes!' Luc's fourth arrow hits the apple and it rolls down Taliesin's back and onto the carpet. 'Okay, my turn,' Luc says, eager to have his go as victim.

'This is ace. One slip and I'm dead, remember.'

Taliesin tries to imagine that the end of the arrow has a sharpened point and that one slip of trajectory and Luc The Shirt will be dead. His first arrow flies innocuously a foot above the apple. His second is still too high. Luc closes his eyes as the third smacks him on the nose.

'Ow, you bugger. You killed me.'

'Sorry.'

They hear a door closing downstairs.

The fourth misses by a foot and drifts into the curtain.

'That's my Dad,' Luc says, the apple falling as he speaks. 'Let's go and meet him.'

Their game world has been invaded and they switch back to real life. Luc tumbles on ahead while Taliesin checks himself on the staircase. He looks at his hands to see if there has been any change there. Still nothing. Through the banisters he can see that Mr and Mrs Daniel are kissing. Luc joins them, unbothered by their passion. He starts pulling his father's jacket. His father brings a hand down on Luc's head and pulls him into the family embrace. Until now Taliesin had felt little envy towards anything in the house, confident that there was nothing Luc Daniel had that he wanted for himself. He can't remember his parents kissing a great deal, apart from that kiss in the faded, fantasy sepia of the wedding album.

Mr Daniel is shorter than Mrs Daniel by about an inch; he has small feet, too. Mrs Daniel towers over her husband when she kisses him. After his tactile reception Mr Daniel takes his coat off and shakes Taliesin's gloved hand.

'It must be cold in here. Is the heating on, Darling?' he asks.

'Yes.'

He takes off his jacket and Taliesin looks to see if his shirt is hanging out. It isn't. Maybe he used to let his shirt hang out when he was a boy.

In the silent seconds before they eat Taliesin says a grace to himself, hoping that no one notices him dip his head slightly to say his prayer.

'You live on a farm?' Mr Daniel says.

'Yes.'

'I have plenty of dealings with farms: dairy farms. Yours is sheep isn't it?' Mr Daniel rattles off a litany of closed questions for which yes and sometimes no can be the only answer. Some Grown-Ups never make it easy for him to really get going in a conversation.

'Tal doesn't want to talk about that, Dad,' Luc says. In the safety of his own home Luc has a cocky and playful confidence that at school never quite comes out. He eats with his mouth open, puts his elbows on the table, and doesn't really listen or seem to care about his father's conversation.

'He took his warts to a healer, Dad. He said they'd go in two days.'

'I'm sure that Taliesin doesn't want you talking about that at the table,' Mrs Daniel says, imposing her own feelings.

'He doesn't mind. I only wanted to know what Dad thinks about it.'

94

Mr Daniel seems to be calculating the situation, smiling slightly at his son's candour. Taliesin has seen that smile before. It's the doubting and ultimately patronizing smile of the Grown-Up; the smile that thinks it knows the answer and needs to put the child straight on something. It's not quite the disdainful smirk of a cynical brother or the humouring, too-busy-to-stop smile of his father. It is more the smile of an adult who's got used to gently grounding flights of childish fantasy.

Taliesin's hands are clenched together, holding the truth.

'There are many things that we can't explain,' Mr Daniel says. 'I'm not one to believe in healers and what have you, but they seem to work for some people. If it works for some people then I can't see the harm.'

'Yeah, but Dad this healer has healed lots of people. Tell them Tal, tell them about the woman with the back, and that man with the nerves, and all those other things he's done . . . the blind woman. Tell them.' Luc looks to Taliesin for some moral support. Taliesin can see that Luc wants his parents to believe and he realizes that his own credibility before them is a small price to pay for telling the truth, however childishly irksome it must sound to sensible adult ears. 'Tell them, Tal.'

'He doesn't have to if he doesn't want to,' Mrs Daniel says.

'I don't mind,' Taliesin says. 'I have piano lessons with a man in my village. He heals people. He's healed lots of people.'

'Is this man a doctor?' Mr Daniel asks.

'No. He used to be a roofer. And he teaches piano some-times.'

'How nice,' Mrs Daniel says. 'I wish Luc would show some interest in music.'

'Are you sure he's not one of these charlatans making a bit of money out of innocents?'

'What's a charlatan, Dad?'

'Someone who is a quack. Fooling people. You say he heals – how does he do that?' Mr Daniel asks.

'He puts his hands on people and says a prayer,' Taliesin says.

There is a long cutlery-chinking silence before Luc speaks.

'What do you think of that, Mum? Don't you think it's lush?' Luc really wants his parental seal on this and Taliesin loves him for that. He is glad that he has told Luc about Billy.

The knives and forks, the finished meal, the gravy stained plates, the clocks ticking all wait for an answer. In the unbelieving silence Taliesin sees his pearls sinking into the mirky pond, losing their lustre and value.

'I think you boys have lively imaginations. Now, who wants ice cream?' Mrs Daniel says.

Excused from the table the boys return to the bedroom and resume the William Tell game. Having failed to get answers from Luc's parents they play for answers, calling upon God to show them the truth through the trajectory of the arrow. Luc suggests this and although Taliesin feels uncomfortable at having things so whimsically decided, he can't think of a better way. They need a sign to augment things, something to encourage them.

Taliesin stands in the corner with the apple on his head. The first shot is to determine whether or not the warts will be healed by God or whether they will go of their own accord, naturally. If the arrow hits the apple then God will do it.

'Can't we make it the other way round, so that if you miss then they won't be healed naturally?' Taliesin asks. His faith in God's ability to direct the arrow, or to want to direct the arrow, is wavering.

'That would make it too easy for God', Luc points out, accurately.

'Hold steady . . .' The arrow smacks into Taliesin's lip.

'Hey, you were talking when you fired. Make it the best of three,' Taliesin says.

'Okay.' The second arrow hits Taliesin in the forehead. Mr Tell never had this many opportunities to get it right.

'So if it doesn't hit now it wasn't God?' Taliesin asks. He prays as the third arrow is loaded. Please God, don't disappoint me, I'm needing answers that only you can give.

The arrow flies above him and as his eyes rise he feels the apple tumble from his rounded head onto the soft carpet.

'Yes!' Luc shouts. 'Ace!'

'Did it hit?'

'Yes. I think so . . . yes . . . well. It moved when you looked up, but I think it did . . . definitely it did. God did it,' Luc declares zealously, with utmost conviction, as if he's just completed a complex scientific experiment that is utterly fail-safe. 'That's ace, that's fan-bloody-tastic. I really wanted it to hit. Let's do other questions.'

Taliesin isn't sure. These answers have too many couldbe's about them. They're not full of the certainty he wants from God. The boys swap round. As Taliesin takes aim he thinks about deliberately missing. He closes his eyes and let's go the arrow which glides into the apple as if directed by a freak wind.

'You hit it! First time! That has to be a yes.' Luc has no doubt about this. This is a new and foolproof way of communicating with The Almighty.

Taliesin wants to stop playing. This doesn't prove anything. It's just Chance's Arrow, playing with God. There is a more certain way of communicating with him. It is as if he is standing on a hill top and can see God over there beyond, in the distance. In between there is dense foliage and a number of possible roads to take. These speculative shots at apples balanced on heads are a diversion from that path. There has to be a clearer, more direct route.

CHAPTER ELEVEN

TIME PASSES SLOWLY when you're waiting for the amazing to happen. It is two days now since Taliesin took his warts to Billy. Two wart-watching tenterhooking days spent waiting for a miracle, thinking about the as yet unanswered prayer. Billy told him to be patient, to wait on God – who is good to those who wait on Him. He said that God was a mover of warts and mountains alike, that there was no detail too small for Him to fix. God could have them disappear in a trice if He wanted to, or He might decide to bide His time. There was no telling. God worked to His own timing, not to the prearranged ticktocking of clocks and calendars or even the unseen changing of a Skin Clock. God was in the past, present and future all at the same time according to His will, he said.

In two days Taliesin's doubt has spread like pins and needles through his body, numbing his belief that something is going to happen. Last night, as he read and finished his book his eyes kept moving to his hands, hoping to find clean skin. The Eleven looked back at him, rude with health, challenging his belief. The largest and first wart at the end of his index finger transfigured to spokeswart and voiced the doubts. 'God's got more important things to do: the universe to sustain, the earth's turning to maintain, wars to sort out, the weather to organize, more serious illnesses to heal. What makes you think He's got time for us? You'll just have to let nature take its course. And anyway, it'll hardly count as a miracle. It's hardly water into wine is it? Miracles have to be instant don't they? If we go now it will be a perfectly natural thing. It'll be because of the vinegar you applied, not the prayer. God had His chance to remove us in one supernatural go but He's avoided His opportunity. He hasn't answered you, has He?'

But Taliesin prays again and gives God a second chance to redeem himself. The miracle could still happen but for him to be sure God would have to make it clear, no half healing. Not one or two warts. All of them. Categorically, irrefutably, instantly.

Taliesin lies in bed and does deals with God. 'I won't keep it a secret if you heal them. No way. I'll tell the world about it. I'll tell them at school. I'll tell Hoop The Mental. I'll make sure my parents know. I'll try and heal people myself. I'll form a gang of healers – we'll lay hands on people. If you could just heal them tonight, please! Come on God, I know you're there, do it now!

It is a Saturday morning. Still gloved, Taliesin is absently reading the back of a packet of oats. It says how food is our medicine, and that foods can cure a variety of ailments. Especially the oat. He helps himself to an extra bowlful. Jonathan is making himself scrambled eggs, singing a song that he likes. Now that he has a girlfriend he has started gelling his hair back in an attempt to look older.

'How much longer are you going to wear those gloves?' he asks, beating the eggs with one hand and swigging orange juice with the other.

'Until my warts have gone.'

'They won't help,' he says.

'I don't want them to spread, do I,' Taliesin says.

'I don't know how you can eat with them on. Why don't you go and see a doctor, get some pills or something.'

There are times when Taliesin wonders if Jonathan really can be his brother. He never reads, he's six feet tall, good at

sport, a help to his father around the farm, vaguely handsome, he gels his hair, shaves, he's kissed a girl, and doesn't
believe in God anymore. It is like sharing a house with his
opposite; someone whose characteristics completely subtend
his own. Their conversations are always a contrary, vice
versa of wills and outlooks: Jonathan determined to gain the
upper hand and abash his younger brother, Taliesin refusing
to be put down. It is getting harder to find common ground.
As they get older there are fewer things to talk about, the gap
is widening, the games are changing, the field of mutual
interest narrowing. These last two years Taliesin has understood this and strived to overcome it. He doesn't want to
give up on his brother.

As he spoons his cereal he remembers the photograph of
the Welsh rugby player on Billy Evans's piano.

'Mr Evans has got a photo of Spud Williams on his piano.
It's signed.'

Jonathan tries not to stop doing what he's doing but this is
interesting.

'You can buy autographed pictures of players in the sports
shop these days, they're not the real signatures,' he says,
giving no ground.

'Spud's visited Mr Evans a few times to get his shoulder
fixed.'

Jonathan puts the egg on some bread and half turns and
listens as Taliesin continues to describe the photograph. 'He's
wearing his Wales shirt and a funny hat with tassels.'

'You mean a cap. It's what you get for playing for your
country.' Jonathan can't quite bring himself to ask why
Mr Evans has a signed photograph of the player. 'I thought
he taught piano.'

'He's a healer mainly. He spends most of his time doing
that.'

Jonathan can't grasp this, and if he does, he doesn't want to
show it. He shakes his head and forks in his egg. Taliesin

makes some tea and pours his brother a mug even stirring in the sugar for him.

'Thanks.' To get a thank you out of Jonathan is a sweet thing and a sign of give. After a minute's silence he looks at his younger brother.

'So does he know Spud, then?'

'Yeah.'

Jonathan is impressed. 'Spud Williams has got forty-two caps,' he says. There is a short silence, then he speaks again. 'Do you want to kick a ball around? We haven't had a game for ages. You can be Wales.' Jonathan becomes more animated now that sport is on the agenda. This offer is his way of continuing the conversation in a language he can use. He can submerge his dialogue in a game.

The garden is an oblong patch fenced in by a hedge. This is where small family dramas have been played out. It has been a battlefield, a tennis court, a temporary home for molly lambs, a space for drinking tea, sunbathing, hanging washing, a space where his mother once threw a full cup of coffee at his father (he never found out why), a space where Jonathan squashed ants, destroying hundreds with his finger, and a space where Taliesin lay down and read a book in one go.

The space has also staged a number of one-a-side rugby internationals (always Wales versus England). The hedge makes an even touchline and the leaves provide a densely packed crowd that roars when the wind is up. Not that they need the wind. When it comes to sport, real or simulacrum, Jonathan's imagination blossoms. He not only plays, he provides capacity-crowd sound effects, commentary and slow motion replays from three different angles. On the field of play his brother is quite a poet, purple in his commentary, prepared to imagine, happy to suspend disbelief, prepared to use a flashy simile and big metaphor, using words he'd never use in everyday conversation.

'The teams walk out into the crisp November air. The conditions are ideal for a runing game and there is a little wind so kicking might prove problematic. After weeks of anticipation the two teams have finally come together in what many people believe will be one of the closest confrontations for years. Playing for Wales today is young Taliesin Jones, fresh from college and at eleven the youngest ever player to appear for the national team.'

It's Taliesin's turn to be Wales, which should mean a victory. Their matches are always superlative, close, and won in the last minute by a breathtaking, length-of-the-field move, involving the entire Welsh team. Being Wales means starting slowly while the English swagger into an early lead. And then, some way through the second half, just as the English begin to rest on their fat laurels, the Welsh come back with inevitable dummy-shimmying brilliance.

Taliesin has little skill but being light he can move quickly and being afraid of physical contact he has developed a keen sense of preservation which keeps him dodging. Jonathan barely has to break into a run for most of these games. Occasionally he'll put in a spurt of energy, just as Taliesin is beginning to feel patronized. Jonathan is filling out his once lissom frame, especially around the neck. Taliesin doesn't envy his brother's size. Jonathan hasn't quite yet grown into his adult body; certain parts have gone ahead of others. His nose, for instance, has outgrown his jaw and his legs are still too long. The voice has cracked into deeper octaves but it has a slightly self-conscious and pretentious bass in some of his words. The physical gap between them has widened this year and that has changed the nature of these games. If anything Jonathan has to pretend even more than usual. He can't put his weight into the tackle.

Jonathan kicks off. Taliesin's gloves fail to grip the shiny surface of the ball and he drops it in front of him.

'The referee has allowed play to continue. The English

pour in on the Welsh. They're driving them back and a maul has formed.' Taliesin feels tiny as his brother envelops him, clamping gangly arms about his body and half wrestling with the ball. This close he can smell Jon's cheap aftershave and that vague bacony smell he has. They are locked like this for a while. Jonathan continues to commentate as he mauls.

'Penalty. The referee has blown for a penalty. Wales failing to release the ball.'

Taliesin takes his place where the posts should be and pretends to be posts by holding up his arms, crooked at the elbow to form the two parallels. Jonathan places the ball with exaggerated precision, pulls some grass out and tosses it into the air to see where it blows. The wind is strong and lifts and sprays the grass up and out. 'And the tall figure of Jonathan Smith-Jones steps forward to take the kick.' Jonathan simulates the sound of muffled Welsh boos and English cheering and kicks the ball.

'3–0! You can't take those sort of risks with a kicker the calibre of Smith-Jones.' Jonathan does the posh accent of the English commentator. Taliesin laughs and restarts, booting the ball towards the left touch.

'It's a throw-in.' Jonathan takes the throw and Taliesin, with no one to contest the line-out but imagined Englishmen, catches it and starts to run straight for the English try line, half hearing the roar of the Welsh crowd in his head. Jonathan gives chase, dives and misses. 'A spectacular attempt.' The try line is looming . . . 'He's going to score, he must score, but what? No . . . he's dropped it, the ball has slipped from his hands. What a terrible mistake. The crowd can't believe it.' Jonathan changes accent and is immediately another commentator offering analysis. 'Well, questions must be asked about the gloves the Welsh player's wearing. Even the crowd seem to want the gloves off.' 'Gloves off, gloves off,' the crowd chants.

Gloves off, gloves off, gloves off. The crowd are right: the

gloves are ruining the game, they have to come 'off, off, off.'
Taliesin peels them off. The crowd rustle. He puts the gloves
in his pockets and then picks up the ball only to drop it again.
It hasn't slipped from his grasp, he has deliberately thrown it
aside to look at his hands. He looks at them unable to believe
what he doesn't see. There are no warts. Not one. Either
side. All clean. They've all gone. All at a go. Perhaps they've
relocated to his face. He checks, he feels, he blinks. He's
never mistrusted his senses this much before. He needs separate verification.

'Look Jon!'

Jonathan squints. He wants to get on with the game.
'Well?'

'Look.' Taliesin holds out his hands as he might hold out a
box of gold, frankincense or myrrh to a king.

Jonathan shrugs. 'They would have gone anyway.' He
picks up the ball. But Taliesin is unable to play on. He stands
there with his hands out.

'But they were all there last night. I checked them one by
one. All eleven. Look!' he pleads. Jonathan spirals the ball in
the palm of his hand, unimpressed. He reverts to commentary.

'The crowd begins to boo. "Get on with the game. Stop
wasting time." They're slow hand clapping,' he says.

Taliesin feels bemused elation and the exasperation of not
being believed. How can the evidence be so easily denied?
You wait for a miracle (and this is surely a miracle – even if
it has taken two days) and when it happens it's dismissed
with a shrug by an unbelieving brother. It makes him want
to kill the person that doubts him; he wants to strangle his
brother and murder his doubt. Why doesn't Jonathan see
and acknowledge the truth? Taliesin's frustration turns to
evil thoughts. He's back on that island of the Flies again and
his face is painted with blue woad. Jonathan is tied to the
palm tree and Taliesin is dancing around him, prodding his

brother in the ribs with a bamboo spear, and holding his healed hands under his nose. 'Now do you believe me?' Jonathan lifts his head and shakes it limply. Drums begin to sound . . .

'They could easily have gone in the night,' Jonathan says. 'There's nothing amazing about it.'

'They were there this morning. I checked. They must have gone while we were playing, or during breakfast. There aren't even scars,' Taliesin says.

'It's your kick,' Jonathan persists.

Can the supernatural be so unexceptional? His brother is doing his best to bring things down to earth and deny the moment its magic. He wants to get on with the game, to keep things normal and mundane. He won't extend his imagination to anything as vague and inexplicable as the sudden disappearance of eleven warts.

Taliesin touches the spot where Prime Wart was, just below the nail bed of his index finger. The skin is clear and there is no trace of anything having been there. There are a few cracks and lines, that's it.

'And the crowd have never seen anything like it. The whole Welsh team is standing in the middle of the pitch, unable to continue. They seem to have given up. They're all looking at their hands. The referee has blown his whistle and abandoned the game. I've never seen anything like it in my life.' Jonathan punts the ball high into the late-November sky and walks away.

Miracles are amazing, until they happen. Then you have to share the news with an unbelieving world. Already the first to see the evidence has denied it. Does this invalidate the magic? Should he look for a more rational explanation in a textbook somewhere? Or is this the sign from God he's been waiting for?

It surely is. It must be a miracle. In its own way it is up there with the other miracles, the big sea-parting ones, the dead-raising ones. God has moved his little mountains. Taliesin wishes for the cameras and newsmen of the world to be there interviewing him, rolling cameras at his hands and adding reported weight to the fact. He'd like his brother and his father, everyone he knows, to flick on the news and catch this late bulletin from a small, hitherto insignificant village in Wales. 'Today in the small Welsh village of Cwmglum, God has healed the eleven warts of eleven-year-old Taliesin Jones.' Close up of hands and authoritative scientist pointing baton at the now unblemished skin. 'And here we see the totally smooth surface where only two days ago the warts clustered about the fingers. I can only say that science has no answer to this remarkable event. It is indeed a miracle.'

CHAPTER TWELVE

❧

THE SUN WENT DOWN on the miracle and returned, as expected, accompanied by dutiful wind, inevitable cloud and unshakable time, blowing, drifting and ticking, unmoved by small revelations in small lives. There were no freak storms in the night or portentous stars falling across the cosmos; no fanfares of angels proclaiming a new age of miraculous revelation. Just dark and silence, everything perfectly normal.

Now he isn't so sure whether it was a miracle. After all, a fair amount of time had elapsed between the prayer and the healing. As he looked in the mirror to knot a tie for chapel, he was the same boy. He stepped in close to make sure, pressing his face close enough to the glass to steam it up and vaporize his image. There were no new bumps and lumps and the old ones had not returned.

He has rung Billy to get confirmation but there was no answer. And now, as he cracks his egg, holding the spoon with pearl-smooth hand, he sees that today is like any other: his brother's disdain is intact, his father's escapism as opportune as ever and his mother's absence painfully conspicuous. People don't really care about his experience because it's his experience and not theirs. He should have known better. It was like reading a book and expecting others to share his exact excitement. It never works. They have to read it for themselves. Even if he had captured it on film his brother and father would have been diffident. They'd accuse him of trick photography or worse. People don't even believe things when they see them with their own eyes, let alone somebody else's.

His father and brother are behind papers and have not yet noticed his Sunday best of wool tie, check shirt and burgundy corduroy trousers. Taliesin scours his father's broadsheet for headlines such as 'Miracle in Welsh Village: Interview with local boy, Taliesin Jones, inside' or 'Wart Wonder: World Exclusive'. But the massive events of the world take precedence, filling all the column inches they can. That war in the desert is still raging on the front of Jonathan's section, whilst in between his father's hands there is a photograph of flooded farmland in America with houses up to their bedroom curtains in water. Tops of trees break the surface of the water and with their bulk concealed they resemble shrubs. A family sit marooned on the roof of their house, using the chimney as a sofa, watching helplessly as a rescue boat pulls up alongside.

His warts being healed cannot compete with this kind of news. People want dispatches of disaster and bulletins of blood from places far enough away not to worry them. They don't want to hear about obscure and hearsay local healings.

He expected more from his father. He looked genuinely surprised at first but he checked the instinctive answer he was going to give and modified it into a more considered and mean response. Why couldn't he simply acknowledge it? 'They can come and go like that,' he said. And now it is already old, dead news.

'It's a good job we didn't emigrate to America,' his father says, trying to claim some of the credit for the decision not to go, a decision taken, as far as Taliesin recalls, unilaterally by their mother. 'Mind you, these American farmers get massive compensation,' he continues. 'They're well insured against acts of God.'

This annoys Taliesin. Acts of God shouldn't be limited to headline-grabbing disasters. The weather is not God's only means of communicating with people: for every flood sensation there might be a hundred small miracles passing unreported, relying on the testimonies of people faithful enough to believe their eyes. His father puts down the paper and mumbles something about people being luckier than they realize. He then notices his son's attire.

'So you're still thinking of going then?' he says. 'Have you checked the times? You've probably missed it by now.'

'It starts at ten,' Taliesin replies. 'I checked when I went to Billy's.'

'So, you really are quite serious about all of this God business,' his father goes on, half reading.

'I'm just going to see what it's like,' Taliesin says.

'Don't expect too much,' his father says. 'Just a lot of old people in hats. It's nearly ten now, do you want a lift there?'

Taliesin would prefer to go under his own steam.

'It's okay,' he says.

'C'mon, I'll run you up, it won't take a minute.' And his father is already moving towards the door.

In the Land Rover his father doesn't start the engine.

'Look, is everything okay with you?'

'I'm fine.'

'You're both very quiet. Jon doesn't say anything these days. I was wondering if you knew what was on his mind. Maybe it's his girlfriend or something. Has he said anything to you?'

'No.' Jonathan has grown more reticent over the year and the cause is clear, even to Taliesin. It seems so obvious to say that Jon is upset at their mother leaving. Is his father pretending not to realize this or is he genuinely so 'in his head' that he can't see? Taliesin tries to offer some explanation.

'He's just a bit down, I think.' As he says this Taliesin wonders why he isn't down himself. Perhaps Jonathan doesn't have a reservoir in which to store these things.

They start to drive.

'I think he blames me,' his father says. 'I don't know why he blames me. It was your mother who left, not me. Why should he be angry with me?' Taliesin can't find an answer to this.

The street twists towards the chapel. Some people in black clot together in clumps and move up the hill. He's not seen any of these people before, although his father waves to one or two of them.

The chapel is high on the hill. If there was a flood in Cwmglum the people would have to make for this place; it sits higher than any building around. It looks down upon the village like an admonishing maths teacher, greyly severe and all angles. It's the house of God. 'Welcome to the House of God,' says the sign. He's got other houses, which is a relief to Taliesin. Cwmglum chapel wouldn't be his first choice of residence.

His father pulls up and looks as though he wants to come in.

'Say a prayer for me won't you?' he says.

'All right,' Taliesin says. His father is having an argument in his head – his mouth is moving.

'You okay to walk home?'

'Yeah.'

'See you later then.'

'Yeah.'

'You sure you want to go?' His father is acting as though he is losing his son to something.

'I'm sure, Da.' Taliesin kisses his father and gets out. He walks furtively towards the old people gathering outside the house of God. They're filing in one by one past the preacher who nods and reciprocates the hellos. Taliesin looks for Billy in the queue; he can't wait to show him his hands.

The preacher nods and chats to people. Taliesin hasn't seen a preacher close up. He imagined a preacher to be tall and grey, fat nosed with sad eyes full of love, and wise of course. This preacher is red, his face slants to a pointed chin and his eyes are ice-blue and twitchy. His red hair is too thick for his age and it is swept back behind ears which scoop the air. The preacher sees Taliesin and smiles a smile that registers on every feature but the eyes. He licks his lips and puts out a paw. Taliesin lifts up an ungloved, unblemished hand and shakes it. The preacher squeezes Taliesin's hand for seconds and Taliesin wonders if in holding it so firm he is detecting something, maybe the fingerprints of God. Being in such close contact with God preachers must be able to discern these things. They must be equipped with a variety of subtle gifts for detecting the divine. When he speaks the preacher is disappointingly prosaic in his conversation, controlling it just as other Grown-Ups do.

'How lovely to see a young one here. What is your name?' he asks.

'Taliesin Jones.'

'Are you all alone; your parents not here?'

'My father is busy on Sundays, Sir. He's a farmer.' Taliesin is confident that this is a good enough excuse for his father not to be attending chapel. Being a farmer has always been a good excuse for not attending things.

'And your mother?'

Does the preacher suspect something? Can he tell if a child's parents are separated? Taliesin leaves the answer ambiguous.

'She's in West Haven, Sir.' She is in West Haven and she doesn't believe in God anymore.

'I see. Well, it's lovely to have you here . . . Taliesin. Go on in and find a pew.'

Taliesin feels the weight of eyes on him, looking him up and down as if he's an exotic traveller from Arabia. In the porch an olive green placard greets the worshippers with 'Repent and believe the Gospel'. From the harsh sound of its ending he guesses that repent is not something that is easy to do.

Inside the temperature drops and the air is damp. The

interior is bright and open, reminiscent of a school assembly hall with its two-tone blue paint. There is space for two hundred and fifty which is optimistic because the congregation is thin like the hairs on the head of an ageing man, with large sections of bald space between one person and another. Die-hards sit in the front seats as if their lives depend on it. Taliesin sits near the back away from the looks. He is the only child in the place and he sticks out. Maybe his father is right. Maybe he is too young to come here; too young to think about God. He watches people as they enter. Where are you Billy Evans? They are mostly women with blue rinse hairdos that go up. Their blue rinses don't make them look younger, they merely make them all look the same. The old want to be younger and the young want to be older. No one wants to be the age they are. Except him.

One day he will be as old as these people and his skin will remain up for seconds when he pinches it. The collective age of the congregation must be three thousand: older than Moses. Older than Jesus. Old people look as though they have always been old – just as young people act as though they always will be young. They're looking at him still. They're thinking, ah, we were that young once. Will he notice the subtle drift from one stage to the next? Will he, if he gets there, remember how it was to be young when he is old? Will he remember then what he is thinking now about then? Will he remember the thought that he's having now, and will it be the same thought in an older body? He feels a tingle at the back of his head and an exquisite pressure that comes with those questions.

He's counted thirty people in the chapel and the door is now closed. Billy Evans is not amongst them and the place is cold without him. Most of the congregation are wearing coats and some of the Blue-Rinses have hats. The coats are mostly dour blacks, greys and musty dark colours that are camouflage in chapel. Is this really the place where God lives?

Surely he'd prefer something a little brighter, a little more cheerful.

The preacher wafts up the central aisle and mounts the pulpit holding a red book in his hand. He looks over rather than at the congregation as he speaks.

'Before we begin today I would like to extend a warm welcome to any new visitors'. The Blue-Rinse on Taliesin's right smiles a wrinkled smile at him and he reciprocates by closing his mouth into one of those stilted smiles that his mother makes when talking to her cat.

'Hymn number 707: "There is a green hill far away". Hymn number 707, in the red books.'

Taliesin is surprised at what he hears. An elfin woman who might be a girl were she not ninety, plays the piano with a flourish of nimble fingers. He sees that her posture is good, even at her age. And the people can sing, despite their wrinkled throats. The Blue-Rinse next to him has a clear, fruity voice which doesn't sound like it could come from her frail frame. Only the preacher's voice strikes a note of discord; his voice is loud and tuneless and carries clearly to the back. He rolls his eyes heavenward and leans backwards as he sings, the veins in his neck standing out as if to burst, his cheeks hot as pipes. He sings as if volume equals holiness and there is something theatrical in all of his movements.

After the hymn the congregation kneel to pray, some of them taking a long time getting to their knees. Taliesin's prayer kneeler has embroidered on it a lamb and a tree against a green background. The lamb looks like a lamb although wool is never that white and the tree looks like a toffee apple. The Blue-Rinse's cushion has a palm tree and a dove with a branch in its mouth. She doesn't use the cushion, instead she leans forward and rests her head in her hands. The palm tree on the cushion makes him think of the island and the boys: The Flies. Those boys needed God. If they'd had God they wouldn't have killed Piggy.

Preacher Preece leads the prayer starting with a long silence that soon fills up with thoughts. Taliesin still can't focus on God, even in chapel. Here, where he is meant to; here in God's own home. He is too worried about offending his host to really talk to him – too aware of the novelty; too aware of his body, of his uncomfortable position; of the Blue-Rinse next to him, moving her lips in a whisper; too aware of Preacher Preece looking more like a fox than a fox; too aware of this strange serious place that's colder than winter. He's too aware of everything he can see and hear and touch and think.

Then he tries to follow the preacher's prayers: 'Forgive us . . . we praise you . . . we kneel before you, Lord . . .' All the time there's a pressing in his own head, a voice, somewhere in there. The voice speaks to him but he can't hear what it says. He tries to imagine God and ends up travelling through space again with all the usual stars and suns and the usual wall at the end of it, the other side of which is more space. He focuses on his hands pressed together. God has touched him. God's hands have touched his hands. Taliesin thanks God for showing him that He exists. He pinches the skin on the back of his hand and prays for a long life; for a chance to see his own skin stick for a second before returning.

Preece is praying for the war in the desert and people are signalling approval by muttering 'yes, yes'. He then prays for the flooding in America; for all the families in trouble. That family sitting atop their house waiting for a boat were in trouble. Taliesin prays for his father. He is talking to the kitchen wall. He prays for his father. He prays for his mother. She is naked. He prays for his mother. Then, hardest of all, he prays for his brother. He can see a closed bedroom door.

The preacher is praying for other things: the Queen, the government, a lady who is sick. In his mind Taliesin sees hands soothing these things that they're praying for; soothing the queen, stroking the government, holding his family, touching the lady who's sick, picking the families out of the flood water in America, and damping down a flame in the desert, blanketing the fire there.

The preacher likes to be in control. He waits for an already silent congregation to be even more silent. Is he acting, or is he really waiting for a different kind of quiet; not the kind of quiet that is asked for in registration, but the silence that God requires? Content that he has people where he wants them, the preacher begins, archly. He is doing what he's doing in a practised, actorly way. He begins calmly, throws in smiles and soothing words of welcome and the shared aches and pains of the week; spreads his hands on the lectern as if saving them for imminent gesticulation, then his voice drops an octave, whilst he keeps the delivery methodical and calm. The congregation are beginning to warm to his theme; see them nod their heads. The preacher loves metaphor and analogy. And the simple ones are the best. After all, says Preacher Preece, Christ said let there be metaphor and there was metaphor; and it entered into the hearts of men and made them see twice as much. Last week we saw faith as a drop of rain, he reminds them. The drop might fall upon a flower and give it life, it might fall into the sea and appear lost and useless. Today he'd like to show how we are not useless; that we all have a part to play. He's holding up props: a mixing bowl from Italy; flour from Canada; sultanas from Egypt; almonds from Portugal; raisins from Argentina; brandy from France; lemons from Spain; sugar from the West Indies; all going into making something whole and yet separate: a cake – and everyone has a part to play. It just shows us that in God's eyes there are no boundaries or frontiers. All things come from Him. Even the things that we think are intrinsically ours come from Him. The ingredients and the whole cake are His. And we are all ingredients, different in taste and texture but all making up one thing: The Kingdom of God. What we must be aware of are those ingredients which do not make up the Kingdom. This is no easy task when things look and taste so good, says Preacher Preece.

Taliesin thinks about what ingredient he is. A tiny speck of salt perhaps or a drop of vanilla essence? And Billy? Billy would have to be something important like self-raising flour or eggs. When he thinks of others it gets difficult. Luc would be something that tasted good at first and then lost it like chewing gum. And what of Jonathan, his mother and father, all the people he knows, are they part of the cake? Or are they to be part of some great soup or stew, something less sweet?

A creaky lady with a green hat reads this story from the Bible as if it's an electricity bill, enunciating words with a pedantic precision. It's called 'How Jesus Raised His Friend From The Dead'. It's a fantastic story. Unbelievable really. When Jesus hears that His friend Lazarus is ill He says that there is a reason for it. But when He arrives His friend is dead. It seems that it's too late for there to be any reason. What is He going to do now? Would you believe it, He brings him back to life – and after four days, too. Lazarus was even beginning to smell a bit, like milk on the turn. When Lazarus appears many people believe it. But others, like the Pharisees, who are frightened and envious, get together and decide to plot the death of Jesus.

Maybe Jonathan is a Pharisee. Maybe his father is, too. Taliesin wonders whether the preacher would believe him if he told him about his warts.

During the announcements Taliesin becomes aware of the time and his own meandering mind. There is no clock in the chapel, time is measured by the hymn number rack. They've sung two of them and there's another one to come so they must be near the end. He looks at his hands again and wonders if the warts will come back. He isn't sure now. Perhaps it could be coincidence like Jon said it was. Perhaps it could be in the mind. Why didn't God do it when he was looking? This place fills him with doubt. The unforgiving pew is growing harder on his behind and a numbness is spreading across his legs.

When the dismissal comes he is the first to the door where the preacher waits to shake hands. Taliesin's desire to show him Billy's handiwork has diminished. Somehow he feels that the preacher won't approve, or worse, that he might not want to know. 'So, did you work out what ingredient you were in the cake?' the preacher asks him.

'Something small, like salt,' Taliesin says.

'Ah, but salt is very significant. Small but very significant. Tell me, what brought you to chapel?'

'I thought Billy Evans was going to be here,' Taliesin says.

The preacher scratches a beard that he hasn't got. 'Mr Evans hasn't come for a long time. He always seems to be too busy on Sundays.' The preacher unsettles him with the cool and judgemental way he says Billy's name. He keeps looking over at the other people waiting to say hello to him.

'So Mr Evans is a friend of yours?' the preacher asks, implying that this is not entirely to his liking. The question floats in the air unanswered.

'Will we see you here next Sunday?'

Taliesin says, 'I'm going to West Haven.'

'I see,' the preacher says. His attention is taken away by a Blue-Rinse. She takes his hand and congratulates him on the sermon.

'I've always seen myself as butter,' she says.

Salt, vinegar, lemon, mustard. Whatever he is he is too sharp for this cake and not really wanted in it. He can taste the preacher's disapproval, a vague bitterness of something. He slips away unnoticed and once outside the gate breaks into a run as if he himself were the fox and the preacher a hound from hell.

CHAPTER THIRTEEN

⁓

IT'S THE SEASON OF MIRACLES and giving and Taliesin
has been told that for him Christmas will be a special time
because he can expect twice as much. But Christmas high-
lights the things he doesn't have rather than the things he is
going to get. The double payoff has a price. After a series of
phone calls between his mother and father talking train times
and other details and a raised voice discussion over the issue
of furniture and what to do with it, his father talks pointedly
of Taliesin spending Christmas with his mother and her
lover. Jonathan choruses this disapproval, reminding his
younger brother of the treachery involved. Confused and
upset, Taliesin retires to his room where he reads until his
father comes to the door to apologize, which he does some
twenty mnutes later, saying that he doesn't mean it and that it
isn't Taliesin's fault. His father speaks with the clear reasoning that comes after outbursts of unfairness. He reassures
Taliesin that it is right for him to see his mother and that he is
only being selfish because naturally he'd prefer him to stay.
He mutters something about this being a difficult time on the
farm and being tired and he finally leans in and touches
Taliesin's cheek. Taliesin, who all this time has been staring
at the pages of a book which might just as well be upside
down, looks up and accepts the apology. As a final offering
of peace his father asks him what he'd like for Christmas.

When finally Taliesin finds himself on the platform at the
station it is a relief to be in the no-man's-land between
parents. Here on the platform the past and the future are

temporarily lost to the immediate, the state he prefers. The novelty of travel makes it easier to forget about where he is going or where he's been and he willingly surrenders himself to the thrill of passage. With luck the push and tug of his divided parents will power the train to a standstill somewhere halfway between them.

Other travellers stand on the platform, pinched and pale. There's some of that keen December sun that always comes just before Christmas and although it gives off little heat the people lean in towards it as if it's the only sun they've seen in years. Taliesin pushes his hands deep into his coat pockets, turning over the sweet wrappers and coins that lie there. On the way to the station his father insisted on buying him toffees for the journey. His departure for West Haven brought out the competitive streak in his father; a need to counter the undoubted shower of affection that Taliesin's mother will pour on him when he arrives. Taliesin is beginning to recognize the pattern.

His father gave him some messages to pass on. 'Say hello to your mother for me, won't you? And ask her what she wants to do about the furniture. Tell her I don't mind what she wants to do with it.' His final words were 'I'll give you your present when you get back.' With this his father ensures his son's return.

The grey-brown countryside passes by. Taliesin watches the fields, the houses, the lack of people, the leafless trees. He begins to think about the distance between West Haven and Cwmglum. Forty, fifty miles maybe, a finger's width on the largest scale map in his atlas. Travelling towards his mother takes him nearer to the truth that she is a long way from his life.

Other people's farms pass by; then a castle half-ruined, caravans and an aqueduct. Eventually the dackadacka of the train lulls him into a short-journey-nap, where he drifts at sleep's edge and flirts with dreams. His drifting thoughts become drifting dreams. He rehearses a conversation with his mother about furniture. In his half-dream she is acquiescent, agreeing not to argue over mere things. This thought merges into other, older snippets of his short past and a distant sensation of moving and not being anywhere in particular. Finally he is looking for Billy, asking people he's never met before if they know of his whereabouts. No one knows who he is or where he is. Preacher Preece says 'I don't know this man.'

When he wakes he sees sea, spreading out and away to touch other lands. The sky is ice-blue and black clouds are spaced evenly across it, placed with deliberate precision. Rays burst through one of the clouds that's trying to obscure the sun. Now he knows that God isn't limited to the majestic; that he's also prepared to appear in the tight and confined indoors. This thought comforts him. It helps him to know that God could be in this carriage as well as in the light that sparkles onto the sea. God is moving with him from his father's to his mother's, just as the moon follows a person wherever they go.

As the train comes into West Haven Station, Taliesin leans out of the window and sees his mother standing next to an empty postcard rack that spins in the wind. She is wearing a silk scarf that protects her hair from losing its shape. He is alert to changes in anything she might be wearing. Since she left he has seen her twice: once during the summer for a weekend in West Haven and another time on neutral ground for lunch with Toni. On both occasions he was taken with the change in her. She was more attractive than ever, like a flattering portrait of herself.

Absence has made the heart grow harder but the fondness returns in the instant of meeting her. And so it does again as he buries his nose in her neck and breathes her in, forgetting her every evil and clinging to her without restraint. Any pre-planned ideas he might have had about not kissing her as a sign of disapproval are smothered in the hug. In that moment he could forgive her anything.

'You look pale,' she says, her eyes blinking fast. She pinches his cheek. 'And a bit thin.' He is expecting this routine. At his coming and goings his parents are prone to say things they don't mean. He could be fat as a cat and she'd still say he looked thin. His father will say the same thing when he returns. It's their way of getting at each other, a vicarious criticizing with him as the means of communicating it. This way they continue their silent war.

She talks a lot in the car. She is nervous, leaning slightly forward in the driving seat, prattling on.

'Toni is looking forward to seeing you, Darling, he's very fond of you. It's a pity Jonathan couldn't come. We've got you a lovely Christmas present. How's school?'

'Fine.' He looks at the harbour and at the pastel-coloured houses lining it like the top shelf in a sweet shop. The sea is choppy and flecked with white horses. The tide is in and covering most of the sand which is virgin, touched only by birds that Taliesin can't identify. He'd like to get on the beach and feel his feet sinking slightly in the wetter sand near the water's edge, and then lie back on the softer sand that's had time to dry in the sun. If the wind drops there might be a record-breaking Christmas Day temperature, a white-hot Christmas. In the hotel windows vacancy signs sit lonely in front of frilly net curtains reminding him that he is a visitor out of season.

His mother is still monologuing. She asks questions without really wanting answers. She never waits for people to answer; it's as if the answers will frighten her. By the time they reach the house she's blinking her eyes again and small drops are gathering in their corners.

'It's so lovely to see you,' she says. 'Really.'

He believes her when she says this. They hug again and his cheek is wetted and blacked by running mascara.

Toni's house is called Cliff Tops. It has many doors and brightly coloured furniture which has avoided the wear and tear of family life. It is modern and therefore exciting: no low ceilings, nothing musty and collecting; space to be yourself; space for his mother to be her new self.

Taliesin is more relaxed about being here this time. On his first visit his nerves let him down: he wet his bed twice and broke one of Toni's kitchen stools. His mother made a fuss about it but Toni just smiled and said, 'Don't worry about it, it's only a thing.' That was one of his phrases: 'It's only a thing.'

His mother takes off her scarf and shakes her head.

'Do you like my hair?'

'It makes you look different,' Taliesin says neutrally.

'Toni did it this morning. He'll be home in a tick. Now, do you want something to eat?'

'Can I have some toast and Marmite?'

As his mother puts the bread in the toaster she talks about the delays on the trains, complaining about the time it's taking them to fix the track. She pours out a mug of tea and Taliesin wraps his hands around the mug, warming his hands there. He thinks of his mother having him eleven years ago, screaming and panting and pushing his hot head into the hands of the doctor. He knows that he was a difficult birth because she has told him several times, in great detail. She generally ends the anecdote with an unconvincing, 'But it was worth it.' He looks at her stomach. He came from there, from inside her. Hard to believe she'd go through all of that for him and that he was once that close to her. But now, with his hands warm on the hot mug, his mother talks about rails and the time it's taken to fix them.

Leo the cat slinks into the kitchen, patient and callous, anticipating food. His mother starts talking to the cat as if it were a person. And then she somehow manages to talk to Taliesin through the cat. 'Hello Leo. Say hello to Taliesin.

Tally is going to be staying here for Christmas, yeeesss,' she says inanely, picking up the disinterested animal for Taliesin to stroke its head. But like most cats Leo is contrary, he does the opposite of what you want or expect. He flexes his back and claws wanting to be put down.

'Don't be rude, Leo; Tally is part of the family. Yeeess, this is his home, too.' But Taliesin isn't bothered at the cat's lack of love. What disturbs him is his mother's fluent Catspeak. While the cat drinks she runs her de-ringed fingers through its straight flat hair. There is tension in her hand.

'Would you like a haircut, my Darling? I'm sure Toni will give you a trim this afternoon. It's the last day before he shuts his salons for the holidays. He'd love to do it. We could do some Christmas shopping afterwards – there are still a few bits and pieces to get. Would you like that?'

'I don't mind,' is his uncommitted reply. He really feels that he doesn't mind. This is an existence that can be enjoyed and manipulated if he's clever enough; just saying yes to the offers he likes the sound of. Once parents become competitors they pay you an undue attention that knows no bounds.

'You can take your coat off. This is home too,' she says. 'The jumper looks lovely – it's just your colour. Stand up – let's have a look at you. Yes, you've grown. You have.'

Toni's main salon is in the High Street, sandwiched between a paper shop and a greengrocer. Taliesin tries to be contemptuous of the poor display of fruit in the green-grocer's.

'Not as many apples as Handycott,' he says.

'No.' His mother looks at the rows of fruit and acknowledges it.

'Handycott's got ten types of apple. And he's got kiwi fruit.' Taliesin wants her to feel that she is deprived by living and shopping here. As they pass he sees kiwi fruit at the back of the display and he says nothing.

His mother is wearing a check skirt with a kilt pin and a

silk scarf tied around a smooth white jumper. She has lost weight and moves differently, as if the sea air gives her a lift. She also wears a different perfume, sweeter and muskier than her usual. He noticed it in the car.

'Have you got a different perfume on?' he asks.

She holds out her wrist. 'What do you think?'

Taliesin sniffs the air around her hand.

'It's okay.'

This perfidious switch of perfumes disappoints him; it confirms the change in her. He'd always believed that she wore it exclusively for his nose. Her scent was her person, her fingerprint.

The salon is the size of a small classroom with waiting space for ten people. Toni has two other salons but this is the largest. Apparently he is a rich hairdresser. There are magazines on a long and low table and trays of tea and coffee. The parlour smells of shampoo and the floor is carpeted with the morning's trimmings. This is the place where his mother fell in love with her hair-cutting prince. This is where Mr Rapunzel cast his spell.

Whatever he is meant to think or feel, Taliesin likes Toni. Taliesin senses that Toni is aware of his part in stealing his mother away. But his could-be-stepfather doesn't try too hard to impress or win him over. He laughs a lot and he doesn't bend down to shake Taliesin's hand; he stands upright and gives him respect. In a superficial comparison with Toni, Taliesin thinks his father would win. His father is slightly taller, broader, more attractive. Toni has long hair and his brush moustache and faintly olive skin give him a gypsy air. But Toni knows things his father doesn't; his knowledge is encyclopedic on certain subjects, especially birds. His voice is his best feature. Put him behind a wall and try to guess what he looked like from his voice and you'd think him an actor or an English teacher. It is a voice that pleases a musical ear.

'Welcome,' he says. Taliesin expects his mother to kiss Toni but she busies herself, taking a broom and sweeping some trimmings. Throughout her life she has talked of the importance of a woman bringing up children and putting children before a career. Now she has a job working for Toni, sweeping the hair, making the coffee and writing down the appointments. She also washes, mousses, curls, frizzes, perms, colours and blow-dries hair. And for the last few months Toni has been teaching her how to cut.

In the salon there are three ladies with their heads in driers and minds on magazines. A man sits on the other wall. He is smoking and almost bald; the hair at the sides has grown over his ears. There are two other girls assisting. Toni beckons Taliesin into the pneumatic chair, pressing a pedal which pumps him up taller. In the mirror Taliesin is just a head, his body cut off at the neck by a smock. Toni holds his head in his hands, his fingers spread. He turns the head for a better look.

'How would you like it, Sir?' Toni puts him at ease with his confident movements and unforced willingness to please. His hair is thick and curly, his shirt is lavender and he smells of bathrooms.

'Just a trim, please,' Taliesin says.

Toni is a hairdresser who can talk and cut without the one affecting the other. He cuts Taliesin's 'bonce' and tells him what 'tonsorial' means. He has at least twenty different names for a head and he attempts to use them all during the course of the cut. He even knows why old women have blue hair. He is a professor of hair. A trichologist, he says.

'You see these on the floor,' he says, 'those bonce trimmings; those bits of barnet; those scalp shavings, there, all different colours. Every one of those little hairs could tell you a story. You could find out how old a person was; whether they get enough food; when they last went to have their hair cut. You can learn more about a person from looking at their hair than taking their pulse. Your hair is the hardest to cut. Most people think curly hair is hard, but they're wrong. Give me curly hair any Monday. It's a challenge your hair. You perfect your skills cutting your sort of hair. That's why I went unisex.' Toni stops the scissor work and uses the electric cutter. It sends shivers of cold tingling down Taliesin's back. Then, Toni puts his hands on Taliesin's shoulders and looks at him in the mirror, his hands still resting there like friendly weights.

'I look a bit funny,' Taliesin observes, feeling bare about the ears. Toni really laughs at this, throwing his head back and bellowing at full volume, as if to show that it's his salon and he can laugh as loud as he wants. In the mirror Taliesin sees his mother watching. He can see that she is pleased that the two of them get on. Taliesin is also pleased.

'Tomorrow we'll head for the beach and I'll show you how to skim. Have you ever skimmed a stone ten times?' Toni asks.

'Never,' Taliesin says.

'And we'll look for birds,' he says. 'We'll see how many species we can see.'

Wearing a blue fisherman's jumper of Toni's, Taliesin walks along the beach with his could-be-stepfather. Maybe blue is his colour, not brown. It is a warm Christmas Eve, quite possibly a record temperature. The same sun that shines on Cwmglum shines a little stronger here in West Haven, the low-angled winter light enhances the handsome colour of the town and its boats. Guest houses, some with unimaginative names like White Horse and Sea-View, others with intriguing ones like Kublakhan and Love Nest, jostle for business; bright aspiring hotels called Imperial and Gatehouse out-star each other along an esplanade. Colour lies upon the beach and varies according to the sun, and boats called *Myfannwy*, *Little Moby* and *Starfish* bob on a high-tide sea that changes colour according to the sky. If the sky is blue then the sea is see-through green, if the sky is grey then the sea is a lurking black. His mother must have found the colour she was looking for here. It must have tempted her every time she came. The slate monotone of Cwmglum could never compete with the ice-cream tints of West Haven. Cwmglum. West Haven. Cwmglum. West Haven. I am from Cwmglum. I am from West Haven. Guiltily he prefers the sound of 'Haven'. It is posh. It is not far from Heaven.

'The thing about skimming is that you've got to find the right stone. The stone is as important as the throw. You're not going to get a five or more with a round one. It's got to be flat, smooth and heavy enough. If it isn't heavy enough it'll flip in the wind. Now this one is a sixer, at least.'

Toni picks a flat reddish stone off the beach and arches his arm ready to throw. 'Make sure that you flick your wrist at the last moment.' His curly locks bounce as he springs to release the pebble which skims over the sea.

'One . . . two . . . three . . . four, five, six' he counts, speeding up at the end. 'Those last little trickles don't count. They have to be clean bounces. Here, try this one.' He tosses Taliesin a similar flat disc. The stone is icy in his hand. He throws it and gets the trajectory all wrong. The stone splooshes straight into the sea.

'One.'

'You've got to get down lower. Throw the stone along, not down; like this.' Toni repeats the movement and sends another stone bouncing. 'One . . . two . . . three . . . four . . . five . . . six, seven, eight! Now eight is a good throw. If we can get you up to eight then you can turn professional.'

Jonathan would be good at this. His brother would throw it in a sleek arch and his arm would follow through as if whipping a silk scarf over his shoulder. Then he would walk away mumbling, 'Ten, not bad.' But he isn't here. Taliesin wishes he had come. He might have understood things more if he'd come, instead of having to guess what it was like from a begrudging distance. Toni is not as bad as Jonathan imagines. It might help him to know this. He might not blame his mother for liking him.

Just offshore a large, angular bird falls to the sea and emerges with a skewered fish. It rises in a burst of droplets, the fish wriggling and flashing silver.

'Look. There. Did you see that? That's a cormorant,' Toni shouts and the bird is already skimming away low over the water. 'Ah no. Sorry, my mistake, it's a shag. You see the white tuft on its head? That's an easy mistake to make. They look the same but for the crown. They're very different birds.'

Taliesin manages to get four bounces out of a particularly streamlined stone, telling himself that if it's even then God exists, if it's odd he doesn't. He is enjoying being with Toni. And Toni is more relaxed on his own, without Taliesin's mother present. Her presence would alter the easy balance and create an immediate tension.

Walking back over the sand Taliesin steps into Toni's footprints trying to leave no trace of his own. At the tide mark on the beach the sand suddenly changes colour and their prints stop. They take a long look at the sea. Taliesin asks Toni if he loves his mother.

'Yes, I do. Very much. Very much.'

'Are you going to keep her here?'

Toni laughs. 'I'm not making her stay.'

'I don't mind if you keep her here. This is a nice place. I don't blame her for wanting to live here.'

Toni is quiet for a bit. Then he asks, 'What about you? What do you want?' Taliesin is surprised that he is entitled to an opinion.

'I don't mind. If she doesn't love my father then maybe she shouldn't stay with him.'

'What about your father, what does he think?' Toni asks.

'He thinks that she will come back.'

'Do you think she will?'

'No. Not any more.'

Sometimes he sees his parents as people rather than parents. He once thought that they were well suited simply because they were together; they must have been suited, they were together weren't they? They were his parents. Seen apart he can see the differences more clearly, like the subtle differences between birds. Just as they leave the beach, Toni points at the sky and hails a white bird with black lines on its wings.

'Look at this. It's a Manx Shearwater.'

The bird sits in the sky motionless, like a star, it's wings unflapping. It just hovers in the wind, supported by it. The bird looks directionless and lost, almost as if it has forgotten where it lives. It hangs in the air and peers down on the world, letting the wind blow it where it will.

Later that evening as his mother cooks dinner, Taliesin wanders through the house. 'It's your home,' his mother said to him. 'Toni wants you to treat it as your own.'

Despite this encouragement, Taliesin can't fully respond to this invitation. Although he feels more comfortable than he did on his first visit, he cannot help himself treading along the landing like a guest, warily and with respect. If this were his home he would walk with greater certainty.

His mother's 'new' bedroom is open. He enters and presses the bed. It's harder than his father's and wider. His mother's nightgown is folded over the pillow, next to Toni's pyjamas. It seems odd that those intimate clothes can rest so casually next to another man's. And yet, Toni says he loves his mother. Doesn't that give him the right to lay his pyjamas there?

He opens the chest of drawers and sees his mother's lingerie all there. The same lingerie in a different house, but still the same lingerie. The same mother in a different house, but still the same mother. Or is she? He isn't sure. She isn't the same. It's not just the haircut that is different, it's her movements, her voice. She seems happier, and she says she is. Not sad and frustrated the way she used to be. Perhaps she has not done a bad thing. Perhaps this is a good thing. He cannot decide.

That evening, after a dinner of fish using the very same fish knives that were reclaimed from the farm and sent in the chest, his mother asks him about his father's plans for the furniture. The furniture, like so many other things, has become an issue over which his parents can argue their differences. His father, he suspects, genuinely doesn't care about it, but has decided to care about it. It gives him an excuse to keep in contact. His mother says she doesn't really care what happens to the furniture. For someone who doesn't care about it she talks about it a great deal. Responsibility for 'the issue' has somehow devolved to Taliesin. He has become the liaison, firstly over what pieces of furniture are whose, and now over when the said pieces are to be picked up.

'He said you could pick them up when you want,' Taliesin says, not hiding his boredom.

'Did he really say that? That's not what he said on the phone when I last spoke to him,' his mother says.

He noticed that his mother drank a lot of white wine with her fish during dinner. An asperity has seeped into her voice. Taliesin can't actually remember his father's message verbatim; at the time he was too excited at the prospect of the journey to remember any important information.

'It's not really that important,' his mother goes on. 'As you say Toni, they're only things. It would just be nice to know that's all. We need a chest of drawers. And the cabinet was a wedding present from my aunt, not his. I suppose we can wait until March. We could pick them up then.' She looks to Toni for support but he wants no part of it.

'Now, let's enjoy our Christmas Eve shall we,' she says rhetorically, forgetting that she was the one who brought up the subject in the first place. And then, unable to drop it completely she says to Toni, 'I could hire a van, couldn't I, Darling? There are only three pieces: the two chests of drawers and the cabinet. I'm going to leave the piano – Tally needs the piano.'

For her 'Darling' has always been a term of endearment reserved for a few. When she Darlings Toni it shows how far she's committed to him. Looking at her now Taliesin imagines she's been here all her life. It's as if she never lived in Cwmglum; never married his father; never laid a different table; never bought fruit from another greengrocers. It's almost as if she never had him eleven years ago, screaming, panting and pushing him into the hands of the doctor.

Toni nods. 'You could drive over one Sunday. Whenever.'

Satisfied, his mother remembers other things.

'Tally, you still haven't told me about school, or how your piano lessons are going.'

His 'fine' in the car, after being picked up from the station, clearly wasn't expansive enough. To avoid the issue of the piano he starts with school.

'It's okay. We've got Mr Davies this year. He's not as strict as the others.'

'We had a Mr Davies at my school,' Toni says. 'He used to teach chemistry. He had yellow hair and we used to think he'd got it from drinking acid. Acid Man. That's what we called him. We all had nicknames. Do you have a nickname?'

'Worm.'

'They don't still call you that, do they?' his mother asks.

'I don't mind it. Everyone has a nickname at school. It's the way it is. My name isn't too bad.'

'Tell us some of the bad ones,' Toni encourages.

Taliesin vets the names for adult consumption.

'Craphead Johnson. Dribble, he teaches games. Mantis.

131

Loopy Lewis. The headmaster is called Caesar. Not all of them have names. I like to give people my own names, in my head. I call my friend Luc The Shirt because his shirt is always out, but no one else calls him that. I like to give everyone a name,' Taliesin says.

'Have you given me one yet?' Toni asks.

'I call you Mr Rapunzel.'

Toni smiles, uncertain if this is good. Taliesin blushes. He isn't sure if he wants to explain. His mother laughs.

'Wasn't Rapunzel the princess with all the hair?' she asks.

'Yes,' Taliesin replies.

'So that makes me Mrs Rapunzel, then?'

Taliesin simply nods. Then his mother changes the subject.

'Your father chose your name from a book he was reading by a Welsh poet at the time I was pregnant. I wanted to call you David, but he insisted on Taliesin. He wanted you to have a head start in life and he thought an unusual name would help. I think it was probably a good thing. You seem like a Taliesin. More a Taliesin than a David. That was one of your father's better ideas.'

'It would be good to trace names back to the first time they were used,' Toni says. 'Imagine the very first time someone used your name. Even Toni must have been new once. It must have sounded strange, even exotic.'

'How are the piano lessons?' his mother asks. She was never good at picking up a thread and weaving it.

'They're fine.'

'Are you going to play me a carol?'

Taliesin starts to pick the skin around his fingers.

'I haven't forgotten your promise,' she says.

'I didn't promise, Mum. I said I would try and learn one. I haven't really done it.'

'Speaking of carols, how about going to Midnight Mass and singing some,' Toni cuts in. 'It starts at eleven doesn't it?'

'Oh, but it's always full of drunks,' his mother says.

'What is Midnight Mass?' Taliesin asks, thinking that it must be something illegal.

'It's just a good singsong,' Toni partially explains.

'You two can go if you like. I've plenty to do.' She picks up and waves some wrapping paper. Toni puts his hands on her hips and kisses her on the cheek, quickly, as though aware of Taliesin watching. But Taliesin's mother holds Toni's hands on her hips insistently and angles her head to kiss him slowly. Taliesin watches and feels himself become transparent.

The church is tall, spired and floodlit, busting with a flushed crowd of people who look happy and ready to sing.

'I'm not one for church but I like to sing,' Toni says.

Taliesin yawns from excitement. It is late for him but the novelty of being up at this hour makes him feel fully awake, as though he could go right through to Boxing Day without a break.

The church is four or five times the size of chapel and the atmosphere distinctly celebratory. The congregation sing the brilliant tunes of Christmas and the words echo in the vault and carry into the beginning of each verse in fugue. Toni has a high voice which falters slightly and he keeps checking his carol sheet, uncertain of the words. After the first carol he whispers to Taliesin.

'Your mother should have come – she'd have loved it.'

After the service the people leave the church still humming the refrain of 'Hark, The Herald-Angels Sing'. The night sky is clustered with bodies of stars, fantastically clear. In the square there is a man with a bottle in his hand wearing at least three coats. He is shouting at the leaving crowd.

'Christ is born today. Oh hear ye, oh hear ye. A little baby, just a little little thing. I saw three ships come sailing by.' He takes a swig from a bottle that is wrapped in a brown bag.

'Merry Very Christmas. Just a small itsy little baby thing

133

that Jesus, smaller than a button. Oh I saw three ships . . .'
The drunken man sways as he examines one of his buttons on
one of his three coats.

'Just an itsy-bitsy button,' he says, swaying. He holds out
his hand and illustrates itsy-bitsy with his thumb and fore-
finger. Then he turns and points theatrically. 'But you don't
believe. There are no believers! Where are you all?'

'He's just the local nutter,' Toni says. He puts a protective
arm about Taliesin. Taliesin has never seen a man this drunk
before and he wants to look and hear what he is saying. The
man suddenly points in his direction. 'You! What do you
believe then?' he screams. Toni is pulling him away now,
shielding him from potential abuse. The man waits for his
answer, 'Well?' Then he swings round violently and turns his
anger on another group leaving the church. 'Baby Jesus!' he
screams and they jump and laugh nervously at him. 'He's in
here, not in there!' he says, pointing to his bottle before
laughing a ludicrous pirate laugh. Taliesin can't quite see
whether he is pointing at his own chest or the bottle the
gestures are so imprecise. The people walk a wide arc past
him and the man rants a little at the pavement apparently
getting more sense from it.

In the night Taliesin hears voices. He is lying in bed,
waiting for his bladder and his stocking to fill up. He can hear
his mother's loud whispers and the deeper responses from
Toni. When he goes to the toilet he hears his mother laughing
and a bed squeaking. There is something conspiratorial in
that laugh of his mother's; something private. He aims his
piss at the side of the bowl and doesn't flush so as not to be
heard; he tiptoes back to his bed and pulls the blankets up
over his nose. For what seems hours he listens to the wind
groaning through the open-plan house or is that his mother
moaning? He lies wide awake and thinks of the man in the
street, declaiming abuse and praise in equal measure and
questioning the people's belief. That man had looked at him

and asked him a question. Drunk or not, the question had a sober intent.

He hears footsteps along the landing and a light is switched on. His door is pushed open, slow and even. He closes his eyes and plays the game, feigning sleep while Christmas unloads itself on his bed. As the last of the parcels is placed he can feel the heat and smell, the unadulterated smell of his mother. Her usually pristine hair is tumbled. She turns towards him and he closes his eyes, before she sees him. She kisses him softly on the forehead and he receives it, pretending not to notice.

CHAPTER FOURTEEN

❧

SNOW FALLS on the ground and then upon itself, snow on snow on snow. It falls steadily, resolved to the task of making everything white. It softens sounds and deadens fingers and for a time it stops the returning train in its tracks.

The delay is good. It suspends him once again between homes with people he doesn't know. Like thunder, the snow throws everyone together in common awe, moving complete strangers to talk as friends. The people in the carriage chatter and peer into the whiteness and speculate as to its depth and the time it will take to turn to slush. The Man On The Telly will have much to say. This snow has come as a suprise and will have caught him out again. Only days ago Taliesin was leaving prints in the sand while the sun warmed his back. Today his feet sink into soft snow, snow that's made from rain sucked from the sea, the same sea that washed over his footprints in the sand.

A beardless man waits at Prescelli Station. He is the same shape and size as his father and wearing the same short coat with the split collar. He's not even wearing gloves. The man comes to greet him and Taliesin sees his father's smile. His father is glad to see him; his hug is long and deliberate and it says you belong with me.

'How about this weather then,' he says.

On the way home his father talks while Taliesin readjusts to new but old smells, sounds and things. His father tries to race past the awkward catching-up moment with short questions and quick replies that fail to conceal a tension.

'What happened to your hair? he asks.

'Toni cut it,' Taliesin says. Taliesin's life spans a hundred haircuts and this is the first to draw an opinion from his father.

'I thought he cut ladies hair?'

'He does unisex now.'

'He does, does he?' There is thinly disguised contempt in this and an innuendo that Taliesin understands. His father makes amends a little with his, 'It isn't too bad actually – a bit short at the back,' then he takes a hand from the steering wheel and caresses his clean jaw.

'What do you think of my trim?' he asks.

'I liked it better before,' Taliesin says.

'You think it suited me then?'

'It made you look like one of the three wise men.'

'Maybe I should have kept it.' His father slows down in respect for the conditions. 'I don't suppose you had a white Christmas by the sea?'

'It was sunny,' Taliesin said.

'You really missed something here,' his father says. 'Jonathan built a snowman with Rachael.'

It's hard to imagine Jonathan constructing a man of snow of his own accord. His girlfriend must have instigated it. Jonathan's girlfriend is more intelligent than Jonathan although she doesn't seem to mind the difference. Rachael has an opinion on most things, especially herself. Taliesin found her self-confidence irritating. He particularly disliked the way her eyes looked as though they understood you. Because he is a younger brother she seems to think he is an easy confidante. She's fond of saying that they are lucky to have parents who have split-up instead of staying together for the sake of it. Her parents are still together and they fight all the time, she says.

As they near the village his father manages to ask him if he had a good Christmas. Taliesin must get the balance of his answer right: not so enthusiastic that he'll incite his father to jealousy; not so downbeat that his father will have cause to criticize his mother.

'Yeah, it was okay.'

'Only okay?'

'It was good.'

'So,' sharp intake of breath, 'how is your mother?'

'She's all right.' Any sign that she might not be happy will make him happy.

'And this Toni, was he nice to you?'

'Yeah. He is nice. I think you would like him too. If you met him and he wasn't with Mum or anything, I mean if he was on his own and you just met him.'

'Maybe. In another life I might,' his father says.

They drive on through the white getting to know each other again. It has stopped snowing and already the black of the road is visible. As the Land Rover turns into the drive Taliesin sees the snowman that Jonathan and his girl built. It has a carrot for a nose, a battered peak cap perched on its half melted head and blue gloves for hands.

'It's good to have you home,' his father says, putting great emphasis on the word home. 'There are a few presents for you to open in the house. You've got one from your Aunt Jane. I think Rachael's got something for you. And there is a letter for you. I've put them in your room.'

It is good to get back to his room. There is no dispute over ownership here. It contains his things and they are arranged how he wants them. He has taken a certain comfort in his possessions. There is a reliability in inanimate objects: they aren't difficult to converse with, they have no hidden agenda, and they can be relied upon not to desert him.

As he enters his bedroom he does a subliminal check of its contents and sees first his teddy bear, fading now but still with springy arms outstretched ready to embrace. He's had this bear since he was one, and still it looks back at him with black button eyes and noncommittal straight mouth, waiting for him to say something. Usually he would, something like 'I missed you,' or 'Did anyone try to steal anything while I was away?' or perhaps a 'Merry Christmas.' Today he is taciturn with it, seeing it for what it is, a stuffed thing. The bear sits patiently in the miniature wicker chair that Goldilocks might have sat on and broken. There was a time when he could sit on this chair without breaking it.

He is drawn to the presents in the middle of the room, and specifically, to the letter, which he opens first. The handwriting is creaky and the letters gauntly loop into each other. He reads the signature first. It's from Billy, dated before Christmas. The letter reads:

Dear Taliesin,

I am sorry I did not let you know that I would be away. I did not expect to go for such a long time. I know that we missed a lesson. If you like, I will give you a double lesson when we next meet. How about Saturday week? Telephone me and let me know. I hope you had a happy Christmas. May God bless you and keep His hand over your life.

Billy.

A year of deciphering messages between uncommunicative parents has helped Taliesin to read between lines. The tone of this letter isn't entirely comfortable. It's as if the writer isn't used to writing and that it has required great effort. Certain words are hard to make out. Although the letter is honest, Billy doesn't say where he has been.

All of his presents are laid out on the floor. He stock-takes the harvest. This year's bumper crop has been spoilt by receiving two identical presents: a Monopoly set from his mother and a Monopoly set from his father. This duplication shows the lack of communication between them and a lack of originality. It's a waste, like having Mayfair but not Park Lane. His parents should be together, doubling the possibilities, building hotels instead of living in separate houses. There's the scarf the colour of a Mars Bar from his mother. As he picks it up it crackles with static and smells of shops. There's a torch from Jonathan that comes without batteries. It's truncheon-sized and probably has a beam powerful enough to shine into the corners of caves. There's a brush, comb and hair gel from Toni, a half eaten net stocking of chocolate bars from his mother, ten pounds worth of book tokens from his constant aunt whom he never sees but always thanks, a home-made wallet from Rachael and three books from his father: *Spellbinders in Suspense*, *Famous and Fabulous Animals* and a book of Welsh folk tales depicting a red dragon scorching a silver knight. *Famous and Fabulous Animals* has the obvious ones in it like 'The Loch Ness Monster', 'Moby Dick' and even 'The Elephant Child'. There are also some that he's not seen before such as 'The Holy White Buffalo of the Lakota' and 'Siegfried and the Worm'. The drawings are gaudy and artless and the telling of the tales abridged for easy reading. He finds the pictures simplistic, the typeface too large and the writing patronizing. He closes the book, feeling too old for it. He puts it with the other books that he feels too old to read.

He has quite a collection now. He had intended to use the holiday to sort them out. He planned to arrange them in alphabetical order, in order of publisher, size, spine colour, title, or how enjoyable they were. There were a thousand different combinations he'd thought of. He's hoarded everything, even his very first readers given to him at a time when it was easier to draw in books than to read them. His scribbles and his juvenile attempts at writing his name are embarrassing to him now and shocking in their disregard for the printed word. He still has the full set of Beatrix Potter, half of them stained from having milk spilt on them in a tantrum over ownership with Jonathan. He's kept the Ladybird books that are graded by difficulty. Next to these is an illustrated dictionary and the once frequently consulted *Illustrated Encyclopedia of the Living World*. And propping the end up is *The Illustrated Children's Bible* which he still opens occasionally to admire the picture of Goliath falling from a sling shot or to gawp at the naked Eve covering herself in shame.

Then come the fairy tales, ghost stories, stories about animals, adventure, science fiction and war. These are the books that kindled his daydreams and expanded the realms of possibility. These books asked him to believe in things: in talking ants and bees that worried about their wardrobe; in wardrobes that lead children to other worlds; in worlds where children always worked it out in the end; rabbits that wore trousers; hedgehogs that danced; cats in boots and cats in hats and hats on rabbits and girls that shrank.

The books that he now reads have no pictures and soft covers. He has hijacked most of them from his father's shelves. They don't have fancy pictures to lure him in, just a simple sketch and maybe something on the back cover about how good the book is. These books are full of words which Jonathan tries to use. Words like gullible, immature and juvenile.

He takes a thin book with an orange spine and looks at the cover. It is blank and the title uninteresting. He gives it the first line test, a literary litmus for reading further. This is unimpressive. The next book also has no picture on the front but the name sounds familiar. It's called *Brighton Rock* by someone called Graham Greene. The first line hooks him immediately: 'Hale knew, before he had been in Brighton three hours, that they meant to murder him.' Who could not want to know what fate awaits Hale? Hale doesn't make it to the second chapter, although Taliesin isn't entirely sure about this and has to read the last part again to make certain. The author doesn't make it so obvious. Taliesin has to concentrate hard, re-read a lot of sentences and negotiate some tricky words, trying to guess at their meaning. His illustrated dictionary's vocabulary falls short of Mr Greene's for sure. Covetous could be something to do with covering. *En brosse* looks like French. These difficulties don't matter. He appreciates the gist, and it is the gist that makes him read on. He's always had the knack of getting the essence of something without fully understanding it. And he finds that the meaning is always revealed not long afterwards. It's the same with words: he hears one that he's never heard before, then all of a sudden the word is on every lip and on every other page and he wonders how he ever managed without it.

This tale moves on effortlessly, pulling its reader with it. Taliesin can hear the heaving crowd on the beach at Brighton, he can even feel the shimmer of Mr Greene's sun instead of the shiver of the here and now winter. This power is a fantastic thing in his hands; a power of transportation as direct as the train from West Haven to Prescelli; the power to take him to a different place, another season, to somewhere that seems as real as where he now is.

After a time he tires of reading and the book loses its hold over him. He finds his mind drifting back into his own world. Books, so long his protection and escape, no longer provide the only excitement in his life. Since that day early in September, when the sun was lazing around and the new teacher asked them to raise their hands if they believed in God, a change has taken place in his life. The potential and possibility that books conjure and weave is attainable in his own life. His own life has taken on a meaning that hitherto only characters in well-structured books seemed to possess. He too can look for the significance in things; he too can uncover the fantastic; he too can go down to the dark, grey greasy banks of the Limpopo river and dip his nose into its murky waters. The magic he has encountered compares favourably with the magic he has found in books. Doing is more enjoyable than spectating. He doesn't have to seek magic in books, or live vicariously the lives of their characters. These things he can experience for himself. He can enjoy his own journey, form his own gang, find his own wonder.

He'd like to form his own gang. When he read about the Flies and their spiral into evil he wanted to be there with them, to offer an alternative way. He would have formed a gang of believers and shown them a way out. He can still do this. The gang's purpose would be simple: they'd pray for people by laying hands on them. Of course, they would need certain rules: entrance would depend on the belief of the applicant. Kids whose parents were divorced would be shown special preference. As a sign of intent they could learn the first line of the Bible. They could meet beneath The Tall Tree and start with small stuff: colds, head-aches, even warts. When they'd cracked the minor diseases they could move onto the heavier things.

He would have to be its leader. Leaders need to keep a certain distance. They must embody the beliefs of the gang and not show favouritism to any member. It would be his job to persuade others to join. But this wouldn't be difficult; the gang would grow quickly because of the miracles they performed. Their fame would be noised abroad by word of mouth until finally the newspapers would do an article on them. His own brother and father would pick up their Sunday papers and read all about them.

The gang would need a name – so important in the world of gangs. Nothing with a number as part of the name – their numbers would be changing constantly. It would have to be attractive enough to win over the tougher elements of the playground. He thinks of a few and assesses their relative merits. The Magic Workers? Crass and off-putting. The Healers? Not bad, a bit specific. The Charmers? It would be misunderstood. The Believers? That has an intrigue and a force about it. Yes, The Believers. It is a news-capturing name. A name to conjure with. A name that would draw his eye if it adorned a book cover.

CHAPTER FIFTEEN

THE RESOLUTIONS HE MADE are proving over-ambitious – and this is only the second week of January. He hasn't yet practised a single scale; he hasn't prayed once for his enemies; and he hasn't thanked anyone for his presents. He is, however, about to fulfil his first resolution – to gather his disciples around him and begin the work of The Believers.

Today will be A.B.1.

It is a good day to begin: the snow has cleared and the skies with it. Under the blue canopy the playing field is clearer than an auntie's diamond. The Tall Tree, which is still leafless, has an old graffito, crudely carved in jagged letters. It says 'Worm has Worts.' It's the handiwork of Hooper, no question. The spelling gives it away. The spelling, and the way the letters slant back and forth without discipline. But it's out of date now; it's history. Taliesin would like the facts to be put straight and the truth to be remembered. If this tree is to be an accurate record of the loves and lives of the school then it deserves a faithful chronicler, someone prepared to update and revise the information. With a respect for the truth and a ten pence piece Taliesin starts to scrape a corrective addition to the statement. He changes the 's' of the has to a 'd'.

Taliesin is waiting for the right moment. The others are gathered about the tree with him. Luc has two jumpers, gloves and a hat on – all presents. John Morgan, whose parents might be divorcing, is reading a book by someone called Laurie Lee (could be a man or a woman). Apparently it's about a boy who wakes up one morning and decides to walk to Spain. Taliesin has brought his *Illustrated Bible* with him. He has decided that all members of the gang will have to swear on this book and memorize its first line – something that, as leader, he must do first. 'In the beginning God created the heaven and the earth,' he recites to himself. This book offers good advice for gangs starting out. It bristles with factions – Philistines, Pharisees, Sadducees, Hittites, Israelites: people arguing and killing each other. The key seems to lie in having God on your side. That seems vital. Numbers didn't count for much without God's support. Looking at his two friends and the as-yet-unconverted hundreds, this is reassuring.

From beneath the tree it is possible to see the entire playground and spectate at all the games being played there: two girls skipping to 'Underneath the Arches'; a huddled group of smokers; a game of five-a-side football with jackets for goal posts; Hooper and his cronies skulking, hungry for some kind of confrontation. Hoop the Philistine moves around the grounds in his raiment of irregular grey jacket, slack tie and scuffed toecaps. No one has stood up to him. No one person could.

'We should have our own gang,' Taliesin says, watching Hooper and his entourage patrolling, sensing that now is as good a time as any to announce his intentions.

'Ace idea. Let's make one,' Luc The Convert says.

'What shall we call it?' John Morgan asks.

'I've thought of a name,' Taliesin says, feeling his way into leadership. 'But first we need to have a reason. There is no point in having a gang just for the sake of it. We need to have aims.'

'What sort of things?' Luc asks.

Taliesin puts a finishing touch to his carving in the bark.

'I'd like a gang that tried to perform miracles, to prove that God existed. Only people who believed in God could join.'

'It won't be a very big gang,' John Morgan points out.

'We'd have to prove that God exists to get more people,' Taliesin says.

'We could try the apple on the head,' Luc says.

'That didn't really prove anything. We'd have to do something more obvious. We'd have to pray for someone to get healed of an illness or something. Someone here at school.'

'We can't do that, can we?' John Morgan asks.

'Anyone can do it.'

Taliesin tries to make himself into Billy, thinking his thoughts, saying his sayings, egging himself on with the healer's image in his mind.

'I thought you had to be a preacher to pray for people,' John Morgan goes on.

'Anyone can pray to God. You don't need any qualifications,' Taliesin says.

'The Magic Three,' Luc says.

'No numbers. Everyone calls themselves the "Something Four" or the "Something Seven". I've thought of the name: The Believers.'

'Yeah, The Believers. I like that,' Luc says.

'Who's got something wrong with them that we could try?' John Morgan asks, putting his book down.

'We could try William Jones; he's a diabetic,' Luc says. 'They say he'll have it for the rest of his life.'

Taliesin feels the leadership of this new gang falling to him without dispute – no dual with spears in front of fires is necessary. He is, after all, the one who believed first: Luc needed proof before he'd believe and John Morgan was always doubtful about the warts. If his leadership is to work he will need to lay down the rules in stone or bark. And they have to be answerable to something: a code, a higher authority, beyond just him. Like the boys on that island, they need their conch shell. Taliesin takes out his Bible from his satchel.

'Everyone should have a Bible, although it's okay if you

haven't read it. I've only read some parts. We should learn the first line and have it as a kind of code. We can meet under The Tall Tree twice a week during lunch and heal someone by laying hands on them. People with divorced parents will be given special entry, providing that they believe.'

'Shouldn't we start with something easier than diabetics? Shouldn't we start with flu, or something? Or maybe someone has got a wart we could try,' John Morgan says.

'A wart isn't big enough. It isn't a big deal any more,' Luc says. Luc wants the showcase healing – the throw-down-your-crutches-and-walk healing.

'What is diabetic anyway?' Taliesin asks, wondering about the number of sessions required for such an illness.

'You have to inject yourself every day, otherwise you die,' John Morgan says.

'So we could pray for that then,' Luc says.

'Only if he wants us to. You can't heal people unless they want you to,' Taliesin says.

Just then, Julie Dyer approaches. She has a packet of barely disguised cigarettes pushed down her jumper.

'What are you lot doin'?'

Taliesin feels his confidence evaporate at the sight of the contemptuous temptress Julie Dyer.

'We've formed a gang,' Luc says.

Julie says nothing as she takes the packet of cigarettes from her jumper. 'We're healin' the sick,' Luc goes on. 'Tal knows how to do it. He had his warts healed.'

Julie looks up at this. She lifts her eyes seeking verification. Taliesin holds out his hands. Julie says nothing but her silence says she's impressed. She then runs a vermilion nail along the skin where the warts would have been.

'Shall we let her join?' Luc presses.

'I don't want to be in any gang,' she winces.

'It's okay,' Taliesin says.

'I can touch you now,' she says. She then turns, barely

148

acknowledging the presence of the other two boys, and heads for the bank to smoke.

Having sworn (with hands placed on the book) to a belief in God and to memorize the first line of the Bible, The Believers, as they have now agreed to be known, move tentatively to the edge of the football pitch where the diabetic is playing.

William Jones is different from other boys; he is well-built for his age and he's a novelty because he has to inject himself with a substance called insulin every day. The responsibility of his illness has given him a mature outlook, making him take things in his stride. For someone who is supposedly ill, he looks fit and fast.

'He looks all right to me,' John Morgan says.

'Yeah, but only because of the injections,' Luc reminds him.

They wait for the game to finish and Taliesin steps forward to speak.

'Hi,' he says, feeling foolish.

'Hi,' William Jones says.

Taliesin finds that he is a reluctant spokesman for his new sect. John Morgan is right. William Jones looks fine; he played football as well as the others and could beat any of them in a sprint. He's probably quite happy being a diabetic. Luc speaks, keen to get things started.

'Hey, Will, doyouwanna join our group? We've just formed a new gang: The Believers.'

'Okay,' the diabetic says, with undisguised indifference.

'Yeah. But you have to do something before you join. You have to answer some questions. Tal, shall we ask him now?' Taliesin nods.

'You have to believe in God first. Do you believe?' Luc asks.

'I suppose so,' William Jones replies.

'No, you have to really believe,' Luc insists.

149

'I do, I suppose.'

'Okay. Next you have to believe that, by praying, God heals people when they're sick, or when they've got warts, or even if they've got diabetes. I know that sounds difficult but we want to see if God can heal your diabetes so you won't have to inject yourself. Imagine that Will,' Luc says.

'How are you going to do that?' William Jones asks.

'By laying hands on you and praying.'

William Jones looks at them all and shrugs.

'You can try if you like,' he says.

'Let's go to the tree.' Taliesin says, wary of others looking on. Their first foray into healing can't be seen to fail.

Under the tree Taliesin tells William Jones to close his eyes. He then asks the group to stand behind the trunk, out of view. Self-consciously, they place their hands on the boy.

Taliesin takes another look around the field to see if anyone is watching. John Morgan starts to laugh.

'C'mon John, we've got to concentrate or it won't work,' Luc remonstrates.

'Sorry. I can't help it,' John says.

'Have you got a middle name?' Taliesin asks, trying to parrot every element of Billy's practice.

'Gerald.'

Taliesin remembers the words that Billy repeated when he healed Mrs Willis. 'In the name of Jesus I pray for this person – William Gerald – to be healed.' If there is power in the words then it is just as well because he feels little confidence in them himself. He keeps his eyes open as he says them and looks at the others, wondering if, like him, they are struggling with this strange rigmarole. Luc's eyes are screwed tight, John Morgan's are half open, William Jones has his peacefully closed. For a while no one says anything. They keep their hands spread on William Jones's back and shoulders and in the act an unprompted reverence comes upon them. They are silent out of respect for something that none of them quite understands. After a minute the oddness that they felt before seems to pass and Taliesin feels that this is a right and meet thing so to do. 'Amen,' he says.

'Amen.'

The awkwardness returns once the amens are said.

'That was strange. I felt something then. Did you feel anything, Will?' Luc asks.

'I think I did. I think I felt something,' William Jones says.

'I'm sure I felt something,' Luc says. 'Did you feel it, John?'

'Just after Taliesin said the prayer I thought I did. I'm not sure though,' John Morgan says.

'I can't really describe it. It was something though,' Luc continues, staring with bright, seen-the-light eyes.

'Yeah, it was something,' John Morgan says.

'Just think, Will, you might never have to inject yourself again,' Luc says.

'We might need more than one go to fix it,' Taliesin warns. 'I'm not sure how many sessions diabetes takes. It must be at least two. We should do some more before you stop injecting yourself.'

'Did you feel anything, Tal?' Luc asks.

'Yeah, I felt something.' Thinking about it now, he isn't sure that he felt anything at all. He was too focused and aware of the people around him to notice; too concerned about what others would think if they saw. True, there was a slight tingle at the edge of his fingers; a moment when he felt something channelling through his hands, but he probably just imagined it. He's probably just thinking that because he wants to believe it. Isn't that what his father said, 'Whatever you believe is true for you.'

Perhaps they should have started with a wart or a cold. It will be a blow to the credibility of the gang if they fail, not to mention a severe test of their fledgling faith. Having done it he feels greater uncertainty. It isn't as easy as it looks, as easy as the way Billy made it look. He's not so confident with God that he can't stop looking over his shoulder embarrassed about what he's doing.

He remembers the responsibility that comes with the job: never raise their hopes too much; be realistic about it. Sometimes it works, sometimes it doesn't. And with something like diabetes there's no telling.

'We should try it again tomorrow.' Taliesin says.

'Let's meet under the tree,' Luc says, zealous for more laying on of hands.

'We need to have a break, you can't use all the power up in one go,' Taliesin says, trying to sound expert.

'Does this mean that I'm in your gang now?' William Jones asks.

'Are your parents divorced?' Luc asks.

'No.'

'We give special privilege to people with divorced parents, and to people whose parents don't believe in God,' Luc says.

'I don't know if they do,' William Jones shrugs.

'It doesn't matter,' Taliesin says, thinking that this concession is unnecessary. 'Just as long as you believe.'

'What if they're still married, does that matter?' William Jones enquires.

'Luc's parents are still married,' Taliesin says.

'Yeah, but you never know what might happen. My Dad is always away and they argued last week. My mother screamed at Dad and threw a clock at him that he'd bought her from France. It was worth about fifty quid,' Luc says.

'That was just a stupid rule. As long as you believe, that's what matters,' Taliesin reiterates. 'It doesn't matter what your parents believe.'

Hoop The Philistine, King of Bullies, Hater of the Weak, Defender of the Strong, approaches with his cronies. Taliesin stands over his satchel shielding his Bible. John Morgan's book lies in front of him. Hooper looks angry and in need of a victim. Since saving his Dad in that tractor accident he's grown more tyrannical in his demand for respect. Most people give it to him. Everyone except Worm, who treats him with a brave disdain that belies his physique. Hooper would like to crush the source of this disdain wherever it comes from. It isn't natural that someone as puny as Worm should stand against him.

'Hey Worm, what you reading there? Let me have a look.'

More pointless violence is coming. Hooper picks up John Morgan's novel and thumbs it as if he's never seen a book in his life.

'Laurie, Lara, Lorry . . . Lee. More bloody girls' books. What a dumb title,' he says. Taliesin thinks about pointing out Hooper's mispronunciation but decides not to. One of the cronies takes the book and flicks through it.

'Hey, look Hoop. It's got pictures,' he says.

'Whorrof?'

'There's a church. And a donkey and here's a soldier.'

Somehow – probably a miracle – the book doesn't spill open on page 116 where there's a picture of the topless Spanish girl that John Morgan was showing them earlier.

'Can I have it back now', John Morgan says. 'It's my book.'

Taliesin is praying for muscles as thick as a Minotaur's thigh. Hooper takes the book from Crony One and starts flicking through the pages, absently. Taliesin would like to know where Hooper learned to be so evil. Is it because of his parents? Is his father a trog? His mother a vampire? He's an animal.

The despot pulls up a sprig of grass and starts to chew it like he's the fastest gun in West Wales or something. Then he lets off his laugh, a forced laugh that Cronies One and Two automatically reciprocate. Taliesin keeps his mouth tight.

'What's your problem Hooper?' Luc The Rash says, probably overtaken with thoughts of gangs.

Hooper doesn't like this. It interrupts his train of thought which was gathering momentum nicely, moving towards the inevitable hitting of Worm.

'You keep out Daniel.' A sneered surname is all he can muster. He tosses the novel away behind him as if it were a sweet wrapper and sees the Bible.

Taliesin was hoping he wouldn't see it – that like a shark temporarily distracted by a small tiddler from the main quarry, Hooper would miss the Bible and pour his destructive energy into *When I Walked Out One Midsummer Morning*.

Hooper circles the Bible, picks it up and almost sniffs it. For a time he is emasculated by the sheer oddness of holding a bible in his hand; he looks clumsy and confused. He has a vague respect for it which no amount of bravado can disguise.

'A Bible,' he observes correctly, although he had to read the cover to be sure. '*The Children's Illustrated Holy Bible*? When you goin' to grow up Worm? Hey! Wormy Wormy Wormy. Why is it holy, I don't see any holes.'

The Cronies anticipate what's coming and snigger.

'It needs a hole in it to make it a Holy Bible,' Hooper says.

The Believers know what's coming too and they rely on their disbelief to prevent the act.

Hooper takes out his knife – 'That's Swiss', Luc observes. He selects a blade – the short thick blade for spiking mountain sides.

Taliesin is saying prayers in the form of wishes. If only he were twice his size; if only the heavens would open now and emit a clear, electric-blue bolt of lightning that would burn a hole in Hooper's head.

John Morgan, who appreciates a good book, feels forced to speak.

'That book's expensive. You can't do that. It's a Holy Bible,' he says.

'So?' Hooper holds the book and pushes the head of the blade into the hard and holy middle, testing the pressure required to pierce it. It is strong.

Hooper presses the blade into the cover and a small split sounds. This prompts Luc to move forward a pace.

'If you do . . .' he says.

There is a long silence – a gap of such excruciating awfulness at what is going to happen next and all of them looking at the blade poised at the flesh of the book. In Taliesin's head an obstinate inner voice tells him to charge at Hooper. Instead he shouts, 'Eat shit Hoop, you fucking dickbrained spanner.' It all comes out in a garbled mess with the wrong emphases, all the worst words he can think of crammed into a kind of swear-grenade. Hooper isn't too concerned with the poor delivery. He gets the gist.

The first hit feels like a conker on the side of Taliesin's head. It sets off a ringing and the surprising thing is that it doesn't hurt one bit. The second blow lands smack on his nose and sends sparks back to his brain, racing through a black thoughtlessness. Somehow his brain finds the time to remember Hale in *Brighton Rock* 'getting it' in the gents; not that Mr Greene described what happened. That's what made it worse: never knowing exactly what happened to poor Hale in that gents.

Oddly he finds himself on the ground, on his knees, with Luc sprawled by his side, clutching his arm. Hooper is standing over him as big as the Empire State Building in America. Capital: Washington. One finger. Two fingers. How many fingers?

Cronie One is standing reluctantly by, shuffling his feet uneasily. Luc moans something about pain in his shoulder.

'C'mon Hoop, let's leave 'im, yeah?' Cronie One says, losing a taste for violence. Hooper shows he's human by hesitating at the sight of what he's done. A show of remorse perhaps? Maybe he'll turn out all right in the end.

'Worm,' he says, bored with his own contempt. Being nasty to people all of the time takes concentration and skill and even Hooper, a genius in the art of dishing out unpleasantries, runs out of inspiration on certain days.

The Bible lies open somewhere in the middle, tossed aside in the onslaught, the pages dirtied, the hole in its cover letting light out and in. Turn the other cheek, that's what the book says: a hard thing to do when your first cheek has been caved in.

Taliesin has words to hurt Hoop, words that would sting and scratch him, pebbles he could sling at the giant's temple and fell him. But here in the playground (a bad description if ever there was) sticks and stones have dominion over words. Here, might is right.

'He could have killed you, you know,' Luc says. 'If you hit someone in the right place on their nose the bone can shoot into their brain. Your nose is bleeding, look.'

'Here use this,' John Morgan says, handing Taliesin some tissue. 'Look up: It's meant to stop the bleeding.'

'Maybe we should pray for it,' Luc says, still impressively keen.

Some of the blood has dripped onto Taliesin's lip and he licks away its metallic taste. Where is God now? Goliath has walked away tall and free. Taliesin looks up into The Tall Tree to stem the flow of blood. And then he looks past the branches at the blue beyond where God is watching without being drawn into the fight.

CHAPTER SIXTEEN

ONE DAY, his mother calls.

'I've got something to tell you, Taliesin.'

It must be serious because she uses his full name. The line is very clear this time, clear enough for her to be in the next room.

'Your father and I are going to be getting a divorce,' she says. 'I'm going to marry Toni.'

It's hard to know what to say. Taliesin's father is only a few feet away.

'When?' It's irrelevant but he asks this all the same.

'Oh, that depends. Tally, I wanted you to know that I still love you. I hope you understand that.'

'Sure.'

'I'd better speak to your father. I'm coming over soon, to collect the furniture. We can talk then, Darling. Lots of love.' He hands the phone to his father. Taliesin's mother does most of the talking. When Taliesin's father has finished speaking he puts the handset down and cradles the whole telephone up by his armpit. Then he hurls it at the dresser and smashes a row of plates, several saucers, mugs and a Wedgwood gravy boat. He looks magnificent as he wrenches the phone from the wall, turning and throwing it in one fluid movement. The phone lands plumb middle and knocks the plates and saucers from their pretty place of pride. The gravy boat was one of the things his mother intended to collect.

After this athletic destruction his father bends down and immediately apologizes for what he's done. He cuts a sorry figure on his knees, picking up the pieces of shattered china and porcelain. Taliesin joins him on the floor amazed at how far and wide some of the bits have flown. One of the plates has cracked neatly in three places and is repairable. All the others are smithereened beyond repair. Not all the king's horses and all the king's men could put them back together again.

His father has cut himself. His father has thick fingers, designed for wrapping around things, wrenching, pulling and cutting, not for the tweezer-like picking of small fragments of china from floors. Taliesin picks up the splinters, managing not to cut himself. Meanwhile some blood trickles from his father's cuts into the delta of his hands. A drop stains one of the yellow plastic squares of the kitchen floor. He holds out his palms and looks at them impressed that the needle slithers have cut him this deep. He holds out his hands in supplication.

'I'm sorry about this,' he says.

Taliesin fetches some toilet paper and presses it into his father's hands. The blood comes out treacle brown in places, turning the tissue the same colour. Some of the blood stains the cuff of Taliesin's shirt. Strange to think that he came from this blood and that his mother has now caused it to spill. Although his father doesn't like sympathy he lets his son hold the tissue there for a few seconds and tries a smile of reassurance, as if to say that this plate-smashing fury is just one of those things.

'Don't think that I hate your mother,' he says. 'I don't want you to think that I hate her.'

'I know,' Taliesin says, unable to fully believe him.

'This furniture business is beyond the pale. I've had it up to here with furniture,' he says. He draws his hand across his neck to indicate where he's had it up to.

'And now she wants to marry him. I suppose it'll be one less Jones in Wales if she does. You won't have the same name as her anymore,' his father says. 'You do realize that? Not even a name will connect you.'

Mrs Rapunzel, Taliesin thinks. His father has always set great store on names but Taliesin has grown used to being called things other than his name. What does it matter that his mother will have a new one? Mrs Jones, Mrs Phillips – she will still be the same person with the same hair, eyes, teeth and things. She will still be his mother.

As he sets off for Billy's a black mood comes upon him like a headache, making it impossible to think clearly. He doesn't feel on top of everything. He's not as sure of everything as he was. That exquisite pressure at the back of his head has been replaced by a heavy pushing inside, somewhere in there. Uncontrollable forces, dark with intention, come on with a sudden unexpected weight that's as heavy as clouds. The darkness builds like a shadow, pushing, pushing against his protective dam – the place where he stores his worries. Thoughts crowd in, black thoughts that cannot rest on any-thing clear. He needs to find some light to separate his clouds.

At the point where his father's land meets the neighbour-ing farm, a spindleshanked figure swings a mallet onto a stake, making a dull thocking sound. A man is mending the fence along the perimeter, erecting new wire and stakes, making sure the barriers between the two farms are secure. Taliesin doesn't know this man, he must be a farmhand from the neighbouring farm. It is impossible to avoid him. The man looks up and seems annoyed. He mutters something inaudible. Taliesin smiles at the man and raises a hand in hello.

'Not climbing the fences, I hope?' The voice is a nasal, stentorian voice.

Taliesin slows a little.

'No.'

'Your father is getting careless with his stock. I found three strays off his land. That's not the first time either. He should get himself organized.'

Taliesin would like to defend his father but he isn't sure how to. He could say that his father doesn't care about farming anymore, that he's got other things on his mind.

'You shouldn't be tramping over these fields,' the man goes on. 'I'm tired of mending these fences. It's bad enough with just sheep bending them. Boys is worse.'

'Sorry,' Taliesin says, apologizing for boys in general. To have some of Hooper's pluck would be sweet right now. To eyeball this man with that manic defiance and simply say, 'So?' would be a lovely thing. But Taliesin's stays silent.

'Maybe your mother should come back and look after you instead of running off like that. I heard she met a shopkeeper. Look at the state of this.' The man straightens some bent barbed wire.

Taliesin wants to correct the man on the issue of Toni's occupation but the real agenda of the remark has already started to do its dark work inside him. He is shocked into silence. The craggy man continues moving the stake in the ground, testing its firmness, hardly noticing Taliesin. It's very cold now. Taliesin continues to stand there for a while watching the veins on the man's hands and pushing his own hands deep into his pockets.

He crosses the field, the comment following him, nagging at him. He takes it personally, as if it were his fault. Then for no single reason that he can think of he starts to cry. Inside it feels as if that dam is giving way and that he can no longer hold back the pressure of events.

As Billy greets Taliesin at the door he sees Taliesin's distress.

'Have you been crying, boy?'

Taliesin nods.

'Come in here. We'll sort you.'

Billy ushers him into the bungalow. The room is glowing from the heat. There are a number of things strewn on the floor, as though Billy didn't have the energy to pick them up. Taliesin rubs his eyes and sees that Billy is thinner than he was. He now has cheekbones and his eyes look bigger than they should – like a deer's.

'Why have you have been crying?' Billy asks, tenderly. Taliesin takes his seat in front of the gas fire. His head feels like a ball of wool and he'll never be able to find the strands at either end.

'I don't know,' he says. He sniffs his snot. Then he wipes his nose with his hand.

'It's your parents?' Billy asks.

'I suppose so,' Taliesin concedes.

'We can pray for that. Christmas was difficult then?'

'It's not really that. My mother is going to marry someone else. My father is angry.'

'We can pray for that too. We can pray for everything, why not?' Billy coughs that cough again, that hollow and rasping cough with no familiar liquid sound. 'I see that your hands are fixed,' he says. Taliesin hasn't even told Billy about his hands. He holds them out and flips them over. That miracle doesn't seem so important now. Billy says nothing more about it.

'I haven't seen you for a time. I had to pay a short visit to the hospital over Christmas,' he says. 'I had to have some checks there and they kept me over for some x-rays and the like – it was an education,' he says. 'I've been told to rest a little and to go easy on the pipe. One smoke a day.' He coughs again and takes a handkerchief to catch the explode. 'It'll be spring soon,' he says.

And just then Taliesin sees that Billy is far more unwell than he's letting on. His once ruddy complexion is sallow and lined from loss of weight, the extra skin collecting in crows feet. There are more than two crows there now circling his sockets, pulling out from concentric circles of age. He keeps clutching his chest and this talk of the spring is unlike him. It's out of character for Billy to talk of things to come. He has always lived in the present and stressed the importance of the now and not the then.

In Biology they drew pencil diagrams and cross-sections of trees dying and coming back to life. But there is no equivalent winter sleep for a man. If Billy was a tree he'd be in his last year and the final circle of age would be drawn. Taliesin cannot imagine him budding again in the spring. His biology book has a see-through man on the front cover, made up of veins and nerves and arteries all spreading from a central canal running the length of his body. The textbook showed how it all worked but it didn't show what happened when things went wrong. It showed things arranged in perfect symmetry, functioning healthily; doing what they were meant to do so that children would understand. There was no diagram showing what happens when things didn't work, when blood thickens, muscles atrophy, nerves fade and bones crumble. These things are happening now to Billy and the healer is unable to heal himself.

Billy reads Taliesin's thoughts.

'I have been ill for a bit now. I have to have my share.' Billy tries to laugh but he can't conceal a wince of pain or stop his hand clutching his chest.

A conspiracy of darkness is shadowing him, pressing in, making his trust in prayer and God seem folly. Where's his faith? It seemed to be part of him, like a limb. Where is it now?

'I told my friends about you. I told them about prayer. But I shouldn't,' Taliesin says.

Billy blinks slowly, looking hard into the boy's thoughts.

'You have a gift. Don't be afraid to show it. Faith is a gift wrapped in many layers of beautiful paper. People see the paper and its beauty makes them want to get to what's inside.

The gift must be special to be wrapped so. They will get a desire for the gift themselves.'

Billy stops to draw breath. He clutches the side of the chair.

'God has His hand over you. He's protected you from the things happening in your life. He's made you strong when your parents have been weak. He's given you that strength. You must continue to forgive them. They need healing too. They have their warts. You must pray that God will help them. Don't wait for time to heal. Time isn't a great healer – whoever said that hasn't lived. Time is time – it does nothing. It's God that does the healing.

'Straightening spines and giving sight to the blind is the easy part. It's healing the things you can't see that's tricky. I healed your warts but there's other things going on inside you that you need healing from, other scars.'

That pressure pushing against the dam he's built is forcing more cracks to appear, allowing small trickles to break through.

'What do you feel?' Billy asks.

'I can't think. My head is all heavy,' Taliesin says.

Billy walks over to him, his joints clicking.

'You still need healing yourself. The trick is showing the things inside to God. Just as you showed me your hands so that I could heal your warts, you need to show me what's inside. You must give it to God, only He can deal with it. God has protected you from feeling pain. He has been gracious – He knows, better than you, what you need to be healed from. But if you keep it to yourself He can't help you. If you bottle an emotion it will ferment and turn to poison, and eventually it will make you sick. Close your eyes and picture everything that comes into your mind and give it to God: that's it, that's right, let it come, let it all come out . . .'

The cracks spread out and the dam begins to burst.

He is on a beach walking behind his mother and father. He is looking down at their footprints. His mother's size fours and his father's size tens are too far apart from each other for him to step in both their footsteps in the sand. They are close to the sea because the sand is softer and grainier and it sinks under their slow, troubled tread. His parents are mumbling but he can't hear what they say; he can only detect a desperate pleading. He tries to put his right leg in his father's prints and his left into his mother's but they are not close enough – he would have to do the splits to tread in them both. He starts to tread only in his father's steps, his prints swallowed by the size of them. His mother's prints diverge and arc away. Then he sprints ahead of them calling out, 'Look at me!' He does a dance that he can't have ever done before; a dance full of inappropriate hope. His parents look up, unimpressed, too lost in their own argument to see. They have things on their minds. He turns and runs towards the sea.

More pictures come, a medley of memories blurring into each other and interlinking. He feels the tears springing up from somewhere other than his eyes, coming from somewhere deep down inside himself, cascading through the dam he's built. They keep coming, flowing to the music of Billy's distant lallation. '. . . Heal this boy . . . heal this boy.'

The protective hands; the healing hands; the admonishing hands; the caressing hands are about his face. These are the same hands that burst through the clouds. He continues to sob, his whole body jerking with the effort, shaking with the force. Billy prays on, his hand a little cold on Taliesin's hot cheek. This touch reminds him of his mother stroking his face with her soft tickly hand, brushing back his forelock over and over again in an effort to send him to sleep.

The memories spool on. His mother is throwing a cup of coffee, his father is talking to the wall; things are smashing into small pieces. Glue is putting them together; thousands of tiny hands work away at putting these things together with such finesse that not even the smallest join can be seen. He opens his eyes groggily and focuses on Billy's outstretched arm which, seen through the milky haze, has a faint glow. He is exhausted and can't speak.

Billy still has his hand on Taliesin's back. 'It's good to cry,' he says. 'What you sow in tears you will reap in joy.'

Taliesin wants to return the favour but he is spent. He rests his head in his hands the way his father does after a hard day. The darkness in his head is like a cleaned blackboard rolling over to the whiteboard. He sees a new, clearer picture. His father is at a table eating the same meal as his mother. There is no antagonism between them and they are eating the same food with equal delight, agreeing that it tastes good. He sits between them and offers them more.

'What do you see?' Billy asks.

'I can see my mother and my father eating. I'm giving them food to eat and they like it.'

'Then that is what you should do. When your mother comes to see you. You should prepare a meal for her and bless her that way.'

CHAPTER SEVENTEEN

TALIESIN PREPARES A MEAL for his mother's visit. It is a meal of fish fingers, potatoes and peas and, for pudding, pomegranates. The grocer said that pomegranates were good to serve to people on difficult occasions. They had the power to bring peace. Plus they were a talking point. If conversation is difficult then the most mysterious fruit in the world would distract them enough. Just eating pomegranates gets people going, he said. Even estranged husbands and wives.

When his mother arrives, Taliesin finds himself greeting her alone on the doorstep. His father is in the loft digging out some old boxes belonging to Taliesin's mother. It's a good time for her to arrive, he thinks. The daffodils that line the hedges are coming out and superseding the snowdrops which have done their bit. She'll be seeing things for the first time in a long time and although he has no expectation of her returning for good now, part of him hopes that she will see the best of what she's missing.

His mother parks the car in the drive and stays in her seat for what seems like minutes. He can see her poking faces at the driver's mirror as she powders her nose and checks her lipstick. It seems odd that she should do this. She has a new style again. This time her hair is as short as a boy's. His father joins him in the doorway rubbing his face and clearing his throat. Taliesin embraces his mother and wonders if she will kiss his father or shake his hand.

'You've grown again, my Darling. Let's have a look at you. Yes, you really have,' she says. Then she draws breath and stops to look at the house and her old husband standing there.

'Hello Tom,' she says.

His father's reply is barely audible. She kisses his father and Taliesin thinks of Toni – the man she kisses these days. Before Toni, his mother would have kissed his father in a different way, on the lips. Now Toni gets the lips and his father gets the cheek.

Nerves make the opening exchanges hasty and unintentionally thoughtless.

'It's a bit short isn't it?' his father says, indicating his mother's new look. Her hair is nearly as short as his own. Her radical tonsure shows off her angular features and frames her face in a confident way.

'I'd heard that you had a beard,' she says.

'Didn't suit, really. A fresh start, you know. How was the drive?'

'The roads were terrible. I'm not sure what time the removal van will be here,' she says.

'Jon can help me move some of the pieces into the shed if they're late. And Tal's cooking for us, aren't you Tal?'

His father places a hand on his son's head. Taliesin can detect a slight shake in it, just as there is a shake in the voice. Both of his parents look at him, unable to look at each other. He is the only thing they have in common now and as they enter the home he becomes the fulcrum for their conversation; a diversion from the difficulty of talking directly to each other. The platitudes come thick and fast. It's Grown-Up speak again, the shady art of not saying what you mean. Taliesin has the impression that his father isn't thinking much about what he's saying because he's too busy suppressing his deeper feelings. His mother is bolder, able to measure her words with more certainty and to look at his father as she speaks. It's easier for her to do this because she doesn't love him any more.

Taliesin imagines how the photographs from her second wedding album will compare to her first. Her expression to the camera will be more assured this time, with much of the unreasonable expectancy of the first album replaced by a wary realism. The smiles will all be a little less forced, the faces wiser and a little worn. It will have to be a short album because there will be few guests and no family there to photograph.

It is hard to believe that this is the woman who has caused such enmity and anger. She is affectionate, beautiful and here. It is easier to disapprove of someone when they're not there to defend themselves.

His mother moves tentatively through the house, re-acquainting herself with the place she abandoned. She looks around and things come back to her.

'I should have fixed those curtains,' she says to herself.

In the dining room Taliesin asks his mother if she wants some tea – the eternal medicine.

'I'd love some,' she says, sitting down in one of the chairs that she intends to take back with her. 'I think the drive took a bit out of me.'

Taliesin leaves his parents alone together, unsure of their ability to cope in such proximity. He hears the door being closed and their voices become muffled. He puts on the kettle and walks back and tries to catch the gist of what they're saying. It sounds as if they are talking about him. It annoys him that they discuss him and not themselves.

'We all went through that,' he can hear his mother saying. 'He's at that age.'

He makes exaggerated noises of approach to give them time to change the subject. His father is now sitting down, with his legs out and his elbows on his thighs. His mother has taken off her coat. When he puts down the tray his mother praises his effort. She then walks over to the piano and sees the score of 'Bugles!' on the stand.

'Are you still practising, Tally?' she asks, peering at the score and preparing herself to play it.

'Not really,' he replies, no longer afraid of admitting it.

His mother sits at the stool and begins to play the piece, falteringly at first and then with a natural facility; with all the right weight and nuance and the perfect pausing for 'the gaps'. Billy would applaud this.

'Can you play this?' she asks.

'No. I haven't been playing much,' he says.

'Why don't you have a go?'

'No Mum. Really I can't.'

She plays it again, well enough to convince Taliesin that he will never be able to play the piano like this. He doesn't have her gift. He never did. His own special gift is not as readily appreciable as hers, but it is, as Billy told him, more beautiful than music, and one day, he hopes to share it with her.

Jonathan enters the room and his mother stops playing. She loses her composure for the first time. There is no doubt that Jonathan has grown since she left but she is unable to say so. Jonathan has matured in other ways. Since he's been with Rachael he's become more at ease with himself, and his 'Hello Mum' is impressively breezy for someone who for six months couldn't mention her name.

'We'd better start taking some of the furniture out to the shed,' his father says, feeling that the room is cluttering up with too many thoughts.

His father and Jonathan start with the dining room table, holding it up above their shoulders and carrying it funereally, mindful of steps and catching corners. Jonathan is marginally taller than his father and it shows in the tilt of the table. They carry it away and leave Taliesin alone with his mother and the piano. She takes his hand.

'Is everything okay? Your father says that you've been a little quiet lately. A bit lost in your own world.'

Taliesin thinks this strange, and rich, so he just says, 'I'm all right.'

Later, in the kitchen, his mother keeps wanting to do things, as if guilty that everyone is doing things and she isn't. She expresses remorse at coming to collect the furniture, saying that it won't look right in Toni's house.

'Sometimes I don't know what I'm doing. Oh God, what am I doing?' she says.

Taliesin doesn't know what to say so he puts the pomegranates on a plate in the middle of the table. He takes one and gives it a squeeze, impatient to get to its secret. The fruit is heavy for its size. He tosses it into the air and lets it thud its weight into his palm.

Jonathan and his father return puffing a little from carrying the chest of drawers.

'Still no van. What time are they getting here?' his father asks.

'They said any time after six,' his mother says. 'Shall I sit here, Tally?'

'Yes,' Taliesin says.

'I'll sit here,' his father says wanting to avoid making an issue out of it.

'Are you happy there Jon?' his mother asks.

'Fine,' Jonathan says.

'This is nice, Tally, thank you,' his mother says.

His father sits down last and no one says anything until he has dished out the food. Taliesin announces grace and suggests that they hold hands to say it.

'It's like one of those old films,' his mother says throwing an encouraging look at his father. The chain isn't completed between his father and Jonathan, but Taliesin links his parents with his own hands. The grace is short and sounds flat to him as he says it. His father bows his head and clears his throat again. Jonathan is uneasy, looking at his fingers. His mother has her eyes closed and her chin triples as her head bows.

'That was nice Tally,' she says afterwards. 'I'd forgotten how nice it is to say grace.'

They talk about different things. About saying prayers, the forecast for the summer and what a waste of money chocolate is. Any silences are punctuated with compliments about the meal – something his mother does a great deal. They discuss the war that's still happening in the desert and for a time they are all united by the vast problems of the world, nodding in agreement at how awful it is that 'this' happened, or how terrible it was that 'that' occurred. They are all working hard at agreeing with each other.

'This is lovely, Taliesin,' his mother says for the fifth or sixth time. 'You're getting to be quite a cook.'

After the fish fingers and peas he clears the plates away and provides side-plates and knives for the pomegranates, just as the grocer instructed. He watches their bemusement. His brother turns the fruit over on its side and wonders how on earth he should eat it.

'What's this, an onion or something?' he says.

The Walrus said that this fruit would get them going. This was a fruit worth talking about, he said. Just you wait until you get inside, he said. You'll be amazed at what's in there. Taliesin serves up the pomegranates as they are. He watches his mother and father holding and turning the exotic, flesh coloured fruits, squeezing them, wondering at them, another of the world's mysteries.

'Where they from?' his father asks.

'Handycott's.'

'No. Which country?'

'The Middle East, mainly. Handycott said that this is what Eve would have picked. He said that she would actually have picked a pomegranate because in that part of the world they wouldn't have had apples.'

Inside is a wasps nest arrangement of purple coloured seeds with translucent red cases. The fruit has a seemingly unplanned symmetry. Taliesin starts picking out some of the seeds and arranging them as if to count them.

'He said pomegranates always have six hundred and eleven seeds,' he says. He starts to verify this. After counting about thirty he gives up. Jonathan, however, lays the seeds out and starts arraying them in rows of ten on the edge of his plate. This annoys Taliesin. Why can't Jonathan accept the spirit of the story? From the beginning of time brothers have wanted to kill each other and now is no different. As each ten is called out Taliesin considers smashing a pomegranate over The Empirical Seed Counter's head. An argument is brewing, one of those arguments that springs up like a hot geyser through a thin crust of earth. For five minutes no one says anything as Jonathan counts. He counts on stubbornly, moving (he thinks) closer to the answer. But however many he counts he will miss the point, he won't get to the essence.

'Six hundred and fourteen. And I swear that's accurate!' he announces, leaning back in his chair, satisfied. He pushes the emptied skin aside.

'They're pretty small, Jon. You could have easily mis-counted,' his father says.

'Try it yourself. They're in tens. I definitely counted right.'

'Maybe no one's ever bothered to check,' his mother says.

'You miscounted,' Taliesin says.

'You count them then, sucker,' Jonathan returns, pushing the plate towards him.

'Not now,' his father says. 'Do it later.'

'Yeah but he keeps coming out with all this rubbish about Adam and Eve and apples and pomegranates and he never checks it. He just believes anything,' Jonathan says, getting mad now.

'It doesn't matter, does it?' his mother suddenly says. 'For heaven's sake, does it really matter?'

'You don't believe in that rubbish do you?' Jonathan asks his mother.

'I don't know what to believe any more,' she says.

'Dad?' Jonathan asks.

Taliesin's father shrugs his eyebrows and eats the pomegranate. 'It tastes nice,' he says. Taliesin's father is still unable to look up. His gaze keeps falling always to his plate. Only when Taliesin's mother looks down does his father look up.

Taliesin looks at his mother and father. Eve and Adam. He sees bits of himself in both of them. He is linked to both of them by blood and flesh. But they only make part of him. They supply the parts, but the life, the spirit in him, comes from elsewhere. They didn't make that part of him. His mother brought him into the world and his father planted the seed, but his spirit is not theirs. He isn't simply the sum of his parents' parts, destined to tread their paths. His life isn't in their hands. His family cannot guarantee him anything. Like him, they are fallible, unpredictable creatures.

Despite their age and collective wisdom his parents don't seem to know what he knows. They haven't yet caught a glimpse of the light that he's been following. They are not sure what to believe anymore. If only he could get them to see what he sees and hear what he hears. This is hard. His family are the hardest people of all to convince of anything. They are thick skinned. They think they know him, he can't tell them anything new. They dismiss his experiences as mundane and childish, as though they too had been through them once. They exasperate him with their indifference. But he knows he mustn't give up on them. He must bring those miraculous healing powers into his own home.

'You should hear some of the crap he comes out with,' Jonathan says, nodding in Taliesin's direction. 'He's mixing with weirdos. That piano teacher of his for one.'

'You don't know anything about him,' Taliesin says.

'I know enough.'

'Jon, please. Leave it,' their mother says with something of her old authority. There is a long and painful gap while the last word reverberates.

'It's all right for you, isn't it?' Jonathan says, more aggressively than he intends. 'You're not around. You don't have to put up with it.' He gets up and walks into the kitchen.

His mother starts to cry. His father gets up to clear the plates away. Jonathan must be sorry because he comes back and helps clear the plates away. Taliesin takes his mother's hand. It is hot from emotion and she squeezes his hand to communicate an understanding between them. She starts to cry more, and as she cries she repeats the words, 'Oh God, what have I done?' Then she starts to apologize for everything she's ever done it seems – things that she shouldn't even be sorry for. She recites a litany of things: furniture, leaving, not being happy, crying. She even says sorry for saying sorry.

His father doesn't know how to react. He can only say, 'Don't be silly.' Jonathan says sorry for making a thing about the seeds.

'It's not that,' she says. 'It's not that.' And she looks ahead, into the wall as if seeing a reflection there. She doesn't seem to like what she sees there, yet she holds her gaze and fixes it. Taliesin thinks of Eve again. That moment when she realized she'd done wrong to pick the apple or the pomegranate or whatever it was. That moment she realized she had no one else to blame but herself. Her mother is blushing apple red with that same shame and while she sobs, he places his hand upon her back and makes the sign of the cross, praying for her to feel forgiven.

CHAPTER EIGHTEEN

❧

'HEY WORM, Caesar wants to see you. He told me to come and get you.' A gleeful Hooper delivers this message.

'What does he want me for?' Taliesin asks, thinking that this is some sort of joke.

'I dunno. But he wants to see you now, right away in his office.'

'Yeah, yeah, we believe you,' Luc says. Hooper doesn't flinch. He only repeats his message. Seeing that Hooper isn't hoaxing, Taliesin sets off through the corridors to see the headmaster, wondering what crime he could possibly have committed. He mulls over the possibilities. Perhaps Caesar is suspicious of the meetings taking place beneath The Tall Tree every Friday lunch break. Or maybe Mr Davies has lodged the usual reading-in-class complaint. The walk to the headmaster's office takes Taliesin through the old part of the school, past the dining hall and along polished corridors now scuffed by lunch-scurrying feet. He passes teachers and pupils and looks into their faces to see if they know of his crime (for it surely is a crime). Caesar's door is ajar. Taliesin knocks lightly, half hoping that he won't be heard.

'Come in.'

Caesar is seated behind an expansive desk upon which a letter is spread, its whiteness calling attention to itself against the black leather surface. He ushers Taliesin to a seat in front of the desk and dispels some of Taliesin's fear with the gesture. Caesar is a popular headmaster with everyone, including Taliesin. He has an intimidating book collection. His office is wall-to-wall books; ten times more books than Taliesin has, and the majority of them hard, thick texts. If he's read half of them he has read more books than most people in the world. Caesar has an interest in many things. Although he's earned his name from teaching Latin, he has taught History and RE, and it is said that he can speak five languages, including Greek. He has a gift for making people feel significant, whoever they are. And he has a willingness to digress, to go off at complete tangents to the conversation in hand. He often gives the impression that the job of being headmaster isn't quite so important.

'Taliesin,' the headmaster says, taking pleasure in the sound of the name. '"I am Taliesin. I sing perfect metre". Do you know that poem?'

'No, Sir.'

'I am surprised you don't, what with your name and your liking for books. It's a lovely poem. "I am Taliesin. I sing perfect metre, Which will last to the end of the world",' he says. 'It's a riddle. Each line refers to a different person. And if you take the first letter of each person and put them together, the riddle is revealed. It's an acrostic; but I've never had the time to work it out. It may just be that there is no message in it at all. The poet just wanted us to think there was. Even so, you should read it some time.'

'Yes, Sir.'

'Anyway, sit down, please, sit down.'

The headmaster remembers the point of bringing Taliesin here. He waves the letter a little.

'Mr Davies handed this letter to me this morning – it's from Mrs Jones – William Jones's mother. I'm not sure what to make of it. She says that a gang of boys cornered her son and forced him into some kind of ritual. Apparently this gang are called "The Believers" and you are the leader of this gang. Is this true?'

Taliesin's first instinct is to deny it, however, he's lost the guile to carry a lie with confidence, and he feels that Caesar is more curious than cross. There is an affinity between them. Caesar is on his side, not the side of the angry parent.

'Yes, Sir.'

Caesar reads on, smiling, as if finding the contents of the letter amusing. 'She also says that this gang persuaded her son to stop taking his insulin and that he could have collapsed as a result. She says that this gang should be stopped immediately from doing this. Did you tell him to stop taking his insulin?'

'No, Sir.'

'Mrs Jones is very angry and wants something done. However, I'm not going to do anything until I've heard what you have to say about it. Tell me about this gang – The Believers.' Caesar's tone remains friendly, suggesting that he wants this to be an interview rather than an interrogation.

'Who are the others in the gang? It's all right, I'm not going to punish anyone. I'd just like to know that's all.' Taliesin bites his lip. 'All right, you don't have to tell me that. Tell me what you do.'

'We try to heal people if they're sick.'

Caesar nods at this, as if it's normal.

'How do you do that?'

'We just lay hands on them and pray, Sir.'

'Does it work?'

'Well, we've only done it once so far. The trouble with William Jones is that we didn't pray enough for him, we only prayed once. But no one told him to stop taking his insulin.'

'I can think of worse things children do.' Caesar thinks his thoughts through as he speaks. 'Perhaps Jones misunderstood what you said?'

'Yes, Sir.' They nod together.

'What I'd like to know is what gave you the idea? Are your parents religious people?'

'No, Sir.'

'Did you see something on the television or read a book about it?'

'No, Sir.'

'Something must have given you the idea. People don't spontaneously start praying for others.'

'There's someone I know. He taught me how to pray.'

Caesar gets up and walks over to the bay window.

'So what makes you want to do it?'

'Sir?'

'Well, do you feel divinely inspired; is God calling you to do these things?'

'I don't know for sure. It seems right, though.'

'What makes you believe it will work?' Caesar asks. Taliesin grows quiet once he has to explain it. Is it better to stay mute and keep a wise reserve? Or is this silence an excuse for a lack of confidence in what he believes? He has a testimony to give, but he doubts that it is good enough for a headmaster, the cleverest man he knows; for a man who can speak Greek and has this many books.

'I've seen things, Sir. But it's difficult telling people who haven't seen it for themselves. Whenever I tell them they don't believe it. It's easier if they see it themselves.'

'Try me. I'm more willing to believe than you think.'

Caesar has a large mole upon his face, next to his nose. It is the only blemish on his handsome features. A mole like that would only need two sessions at the most to heal. His is a friendly face, a face that invites confession. But Taliesin can't tell him about the light and the parting clouds; about Billy Evans and his miraculous healing power; about Mrs Willis' back and his warts; about all the people that Billy has healed with prayer; or about the spirit and the lovely pressure in his head. Caesar will think him mad.

'It's hard to explain, Sir.'

The headmaster gives him a disappointed look.

'I'm only curious. I'm interested you see,' he says. 'You know what belief means? You know where the word comes from?'

Taliesin has not questioned the etymology of it. 'Sir?'

'It's an Old English word: Liefen. It means to make allowance for. It isn't just about having faith in something you think is true. It actually means making allowance for it, making a sacrifice if you like – doing something about it. True believers never fear standing up for what they believe.'

The headmaster is right. In books, and sometimes in real life, heroes give great speeches. Fearlessly, they stand up in front of everyone in an open space and give a word-perfect speech that wins the hearts and minds of their listeners – even their enemies and doubters. They confound everyone with the wisdom of their words, the sheer rightness of them. This sheer rightness is augmented by the timing of the speech – just in time to save the day, to save everyone. But Taliesin doesn't feel ready to give that speech.

Caesar's eyes shine. 'My mother was a great believer in prayer,' he says, moving over to the window to watch some boys kick a ball around the playing fields. 'She prayed for me when I was very sick with a fever once. The doctors were quite worried. I was always sick. But this was serious; I had a dangerously high temperature. My mother prayed for me and my temperature came down within an hour – just like that.' He flicks his fingers to emphasize the fact. 'Remarkable really. The doctor told her that it was a miracle. She said that prayer was the greatest medicine. She always prayed, for everything. I don't know why, but I've never tried it. I have a vague belief in these things. It is only vague. I could never capture the faith that my mother had.'

Taliesin wants to tell the headmaster that faith doesn't come from our parents.

'Are you afraid to share your belief?' Caesar asks. 'Would

you stand up in front of the class and tell them about these things that you say you've seen?'

'Maybe, Sir.'

'Only maybe. You're not going to deny it then?'

'No, Sir.'

Caesar looks at the letter and flicks it with his middle finger. 'Mrs Jones says you should be punished which I think is a little inappropriate. I could chastise you for misleading Jones, even if it was unintentional, but I can't see that there is anything wrong with what you've done. My mother would have praised not punished you. However, I ought to placate Mrs Jones somehow. As a compromise you can give a Class Assembly. Tell what you've seen. It'll make a change from telling them what you did in your holidays or whatever the usual Class Assembly topic is.'

Taliesin swallows hard. In front of the whole class? Tell them why he believes? They will humiliate him.

'I will tell Mr Davies that I've spoken to you and that I have dealt with you accordingly,' Caesar says, with a smile. 'When is your next Class Assembly?'

'Next Thursday, Sir.'

'That'll give you time to think about it. Tell me Jones, do you think we should say prayers before we go home at night, the way we did in primary school?' Caesar continues to watch the children playing in the fields, screaming, yelling and squealing. 'It might do them good if they did.'

The bell sounds for the end of the break. The children are slow to react to the bell, most of them are so absorbed in what they're doing. They move with reluctance, squeezing out the extra seconds as if it is their right to enjoy every moment, and never to do anything that isn't enjoyable.

'Right. You'd better get to your lessons. By the way, how is that brother of yours?'

'He's okay, Sir. He works for my father, now.'

'You're very different aren't you? He was never much of

an academic. Good sportsman though. Say hello to him for me.'

'Yes, Sir.'

'And don't try anything too fantastic.'

'No, Sir.'

'I don't want any more letters from parents thinking their children are being led astray by a young Messiah. We all know what happens to Messiahs.'

'Yes, Sir.'

Taliesin gets the gist of what Caesar is saying. Jesus was a Messiah, that much he knows. And Jesus was punished for being one – put to death for it. Caesar has prompted the question, a most difficult question: what is he prepared to do for his belief? The thought of explaining it fills him with dread. Standing up in front of the class and telling them about everything would be like a death, his equivalent crucifixion. What on earth would he say? Where would he start – with clouds and that funny pressure at the back of his head? With warts disappearing and spines straightening? With dreams and voices? What do these things amount to: a succession of dubious coincidence, or a purposeful display of truth? The fact that these things have happened makes them no more believable. If only they were him. If only they'd seen what he's seen.

CHAPTER NINETEEN

❧

THE NIGHT BEFORE Class Assembly he has a dream. The
whole dream is in lush purple, and is as mannered and stagey
as a film or a scene in a play. His hands are tied in front of him
with a rough string; they are overrun with warts so densely
clustered that they look like the hands of a leper. His feet are
bare and small, still only size fours. His pastel striped bed-
sheet is wrapped around his body like a toga, tied with
dressing gown cord. He's walking up an aisle, between
wooden school chairs. On the left and right are children
taunting and Grown-Ups scolding, raining abuse down on
him.

Caesar sits at the end of the aisle behind a desk in the attire
of a Roman, laurel in his hair. At his side is a lectern. He
silences the rabble with his raised palm, pink and clean. In the
crowd Taliesin sees people snarling at him with a hate that
can't really be coming from them. He can't understand what
he's done to make them so angry. Their anger twists their
features to distortion. He sees his parents not saying anything. He sees William Jones, unable to look him in the eye,
holding his head. Julie Dyer sits silent like a betrayer near the
back. Caesar asks for quiet again and he holds up a letter. The
rabble are hushed. Caesar says that this boy is accused of
many things: putting spells upon innocent people, attempt-
ing to resurrect the dead, lying to people about miracles.
Caesar says that he isn't aware of these things himself and
sees no reason to punish the boy. Although he has the power
to let Taliesin go he wants the crowd to decide upon his fate.

'Make him show us a miracle!' someone shouts.

'Yeah. Prove it, Jones!'

Caesar holds up both hands this time; the crowd press forward in their agitation.

'I think the boy should tell us, in his own words, why he believes. And if you are happy with his answer then I will let him go. If not, then you can choose as you will.'

Taliesin is pushed forward to the lectern. Caesar bids him to speak to the crowd. As he turns and stands before them he sees many people that he knows; a mix of school children and Grown-Ups. The heckling and catcalling continue for a while. It seems they will never listen to him. When he opens his mouth to speak, nothing comes out, nothing at all. He knows what to say but the words won't come. He swallows but it is useless. He cannot teh them why he believes.

'Why don't you heal yourself, leperhands!'

'Good God, look at them!' another shouts.

'Can't you do something about them?'

The crowd sways from side to side and then appears to part, like a sea. A man pushes through, trying to get to the front. Although he doesn't know this man, Taliesin recognizes him from somewhere. A beautiful man with perfect movement and stillness and a look that looks deep into Taliesin's face and beyond, into the core of himself. The man stretches out his hand to touch Taliesin, his hand reaching out over the heads of the pressing crowd, and as he touches him, Taliesin looks down and sees that his hands are healed.

He wakes at this point, feeling wet. He kicks back the blankets and examines the sheets. There is no stain this time, it's just his sweat. The sweat smells strong, almost like the smell of his father. He lies still for several minutes assimilating his surroundings and adjusting to the reality of consciousness. The dream was so vivid that for a time he wonders if he can speak. He says some words: 'Morning, hello, ceiling.' He checks his hands. He remembers his dumbness in the dream and he is immediately thankful that this was just a dream. He now tries to think of what he would have said to the crowd of the dream – what he will say to the crowd that will be waiting for him today. He cannot think of anything other than what he knows. He must trust in his experience to date and tell them of it. His experiences point to some kind of answer.

As he dresses for school he sees that his trousers are too short – even without shoes on, they look too short. And there is nothing more to let down, no further cloth to draw on. He must have grown another inch in the last few months without noticing it and standing before the full-length mirror on the back of the door, he wonders at the imperceptible growth of his body, finding it hard to accept that he will change from what he sees here in the mirror into a Grown-Up, with different voice, smells and habits, and perhaps different beliefs. He wonders if his belief will change, if he will still believe what he believes now in ten, twenty or fifty years' time?

Today is the day he must stand up and say why he believes. He has prepared nothing in his mind. All he can think of is his reticence and the sniggering ridicule stirring at the back of the class. As he does his tie, he rehearses his first words and hears the cackle of Hooper and his followers. It would be good if God showed up today, but there can be no guarantee of this. God chooses when to reveal Himself. He doesn't understand this selectiveness on God's part. It's a mystery. Just as he can't explain why sometimes he can talk to God as naturally as if He were sitting in the room with Him, and then at other times feel that nothing is there.

How can he make them believe when his own faith falters this way? He can't. It isn't up to him. Why, he could stand before the class for days, weeks, months or years testifying and they would still not believe him. He could perform miracles before their eyes: turn ink into wine, bubble gum to

184

bread, conjure a fish in his palm – they still would not change. The ones who listen to him will be the ones who already have a desire to believe planted within them.

He prays now that the words won't die in his throat the way they did in the dream. He prays that his words will speak the truth. It is tempting to exaggerate the things he's witnessed, to sprinkle his testimony with bogus detail and elaborate extras in order to convince them. But there would be no point. God will be listening. There is nothing to be gained from meddling with the truth. If he tells them a stack of lies and they like what he says, he will have deceived himself. If he tells them the truth and they laugh him down then he will have done the right thing. A witness must testify.

Taliesin takes his place at the lectern, his stomach churning up at the sight of twenty-two faces ready to dismiss or accept his words.

'What you gonna talk about Worm: diabetes?'

'Hey stand up Worm!'

'Quiet, please. Let Taliesin give his assembly,' Mr Davies demands.

'Show us your warts, Worm!'

Hooper is one of those in shadow at the back of the class. He is quiet but Taliesin knows he's there. Unusually, he has taken a back seat and allowed the others to throw the verbal darts that disrupt and discourage. Mr Davies orders one final silence.

'For heaven's sake, let the boy speak!' he shouts.

A kind of hush comes over the class. As Taliesin looks at them he doesn't really see any one person. He remembers the advice the teacher gave the class last year, 'When you speak to people, try and focus on a particular spot near the back of the room, just above the heads of your listeners.' He does this now, although from where he is standing the far corners of the room are in shade and he cannot quite see those who are sitting there.

He begins by telling the class that he has always had a sense of there being a God but that he's not been able to explain this. It has just been there. He tells them how he used to pray without really thinking about what he was doing or to whom he was addressing his words. He tells them of his childhood image of God, as depicted in his illustrated Bible. He tells them about the voice in his head, separate from his own, and the exquisite pressure he feels at the back of his head when he thinks about God.

Some laughs but no catcalls yet. The class are not the merciless mob of his dream and it seems they are prepared to listen. Encouraged by the quiet, he tells them about Billy Evans and the miracles he performed. He demonstrates the technique of praying for the sick as practised by Billy and taught by Jesus two thousand years ago. He shows them his hands and the fact that two days after prayer his warts completely disappeared.

'How do we know you had all those warts?' one of Hooper's cronies asks. 'I never saw them, so how can I know for sure?'

'He had them. I saw them all,' Julie Dyer says and with that the class murmur awe as though Moses himself had just written it as fact on a tablet.

'Let him continue, please,' the teacher says.

Taliesin goes on to tell them about Mrs Willis. He looks into the far corners of the class and speaks to the shadow, and as he talks he is convinced by what he's saying. Giving witness to these things gives them a sparkle. The lustre of his pearls is appreciated by exposing them. He ends by saying that, with enough faith, anyone in the class could do these things. Anyone.

The class clap and Taliesin asks if there are any questions.

Someone asks him why it didn't work with William Jones?

'I'm not sure,' is all he can say.

Then from the dark corner Hooper's voice comes over loud and clear. 'Why not show us a healing now!' He emerges into the light with his four fingered hand in the air.

'Not now, Hooper,' Mr Davies says, trying to wrap up the proceedings. 'Thank you for a most interesting and informative talk, Jones.'

But the class like Hooper's idea; they all start to call for a demonstration right here in the classroom.

'See if you can heal my sprained ankle.'

'Fix my spots!'

'No. Heal this!' Hooper says, and he holds up his once-finger that is now no more than a two-inch stump.

'That is hardly fair,' Mr Davies intercedes.

'Why not, Sir?' Hooper implores. 'He told us he saw a spine being straightened and this healer made someone's tooth grow back from nothing. Why can't he try my finger?'

'Yeah, Sir, why not? Let him try.'

Taliesin hears Luc call out. 'Go on Tal, try it. You can do it.'

Mr Davies shakes his head. 'All right, all right! But just one, we haven't got time for everybody's complaint. Just one.'

Hooper stands before Taliesin and holds his phantom finger up for all to see. The class press in. Some of them stand on chairs to get a better view.

'Go on, Jones. Fix it!' someone calls.

Taliesin still shakes his head.

'You've got to try,' Luc prompts again. 'Show them!'

Hooper still has a hand out. His complete hand is on his hip and his eyes swim all over Taliesin.

'I bet you can't do it,' he says.

Hooper was always going to try something on to test him. If he refuses him now the class will call him coward. If he tries and it fails they'll call him a fake.

'I will try,' he says.

Taliesin has to remind himself that it is his faith that matters not the faith of the subject. It is odd taking Hooper's hand in his own. Hooper is a little fearful, recoiling his hand.

'What are you afraid of?' Taliesin asks him.

'Nothing,' Hooper says. He lets his hand be held.

Taliesin says the prayer quietly so that they won't hear what he's saying. He is uncomfortable using the name of Jesus in front of so many people.

'What's he saying?' some ask.

'Speak up.'

Everyone watches the tip of Hooper's stump.

'Will he get a new nail?' Julie Dyer asks.

'Ssshhh!'

'You should pay him Hoop, if it grows back. A finger's worth a bomb!' someone says.

Taliesin and Hooper are unaware of the class now. They are locked into a little world of their own. Taliesin prays again. Come on God, he says to himself, help me this time.

'I hope you can do it,' Hooper says, in a soft, mumbled voice that only Taliesin can hear. A change has come over him. Hooper's desire to be healed is outweighing his desire to make Taliesin appear a fool. But just then the bell sounds and Mr Davies asks the class to go back to their seats.

'Come on now, that's enough, I'm afraid,' the teacher says.

'We can try tomorrow,' Taliesin says to Hooper.

'Is it longer now, Hoop?' someone calls out.

Hooper looks closely at the stump and reveals that it is still a stump.

'What about that man? Why don't you take me to him,' Hooper asks Taliesin, in the same discreet sotto voce. The prayer hasn't made Hooper's finger grow back, but at least it has made him yield to something. Beneath the brittle, showy

188

armour Hooper is pliant. In exposing just some of his softness to Taliesin, Hooper is opening himself up to possibility.
Unbelievably, Hooper wants to believe it is possible.

CHAPTER TWENTY

❧

TALIESIN JONES, Luc The Shirt and Hoop The Mental leave school together. They share the entire back seat of the bus and Hooper teaches Luc and Taliesin how to blow smoke rings. Taliesin can't inhale without spluttering every time and he marvels at Luc and Hoop's ability to inhale all the way down and blow the smoke out of their noses, one nostril at a time. Hoop does smoke rings that he can direct with the precision of a deck quoit onto an outstretched foot several feet away. Taliesin attempts a ring but it splutters out as a blob with no recognizable hole in the middle. The smoke is going to his head, making him giddy. I am here not there. I am here not there.

This unlikely trio are bonded by the purpose of their mission. Taliesin is conversing with Hooper and Hooper is calling him Tal. Away from the theatre of school, Hoop drops his act and admits weaknesses. He dares to say that he is frightened at the prospect of meeting a healer and having his finger grow back. Taliesin feels heady and in his headiness he experiences the miracle of feeling affection for Hooper: the way his hair sticks up, his fantastic smoke sculptures, his sartorial rebellion, even his sneer. Incredible to think that he could love his enemy.

Taliesin finds himself doing what he always does when he feels happiness. He projects into the future the here and now and imagines himself looking back then and remembering this here and now. He would like the memory then to be as clear as the feeling now, clear enough to recall the exact blur of blue and green Embassy filter tip smoke and the shape of Hoop's fabulous, floating, foot-coronating vapour crowns, and the fact that for a few fleeting seconds he loved his enemy. But as usual the moment passes, shedding itself, leaving only a scaly skin of memory. Taliesin fancies that this desire to hold time is happening because he is growing up and doesn't want to. He feels that he is losing the peculiar gift of childhood – that ability to live completely in the present.

By the time Hoop has coronated Taliesin's foot for the tenth time the bus is in Cwmglum and the three boys leave the chewing gum seats and cloudy bus behind.

'I feel sick,' Taliesin says.

'That's called a high,' Hoop The Lingo-Knowing Smoke Blower says. Taliesin sits on the pavement and lets himself float back down by breathing the cold air deeply. I am here not there.

They set off up the hill towards the bungalow. The steep pitch of Billy Evans' roof reminds Taliesin of the lean of the gravestones in the chapel yard. It is made from slate and looks almost too heavy for the walls, like an outsized hat covering a small thin head. A single magpie rests on the elderberry tree in front of the bungalow and then flies across the roof, over the smokeless chimney.

'Pinch me,' Hoop demands. 'Morning Mr Magpie, how's your wife?' he adds. He waits to see if a second Magpie will join the single bird and cancel the sorrow that the solitary bird prophesies, but no other bird comes.

'That's bad luck,' he says. Taliesin looks for movement through the wine-dark windows of the house and can see a faint light coming from one of the rooms towards the back. This half light and lack of life within the house is eerie. It is stiller than it should be. The silence is sly.

'He could be out,' Taliesin says.

They ring the bell and wait. They ring again and look at each other. Luc says he can hear voices and he presses an ear to the letter flap. The door opens when he leans on it. As they move into the house they can hear that the voices are woody, male voices. They move on into the open lounge and the voices become louder and recognizable as radio voices. Billy's smoking and praying chair has its cushions puffed up and the travelling rug folded neatly over its head rest. In the kitchen there are some unwashed pans in the sink and a tea bag blocks the plug. The voices discuss why crime is on the increase. At the opposite end of the lounge, a door is half open and a light is on in the room. They walk towards the light, treading quiet as burglars.

'Billy?' Taliesin whispers.

Through the gap in the door Taliesin can see a figure lying still on the bed like a Russian president lying in state. He is fully dressed, as if going to chapel or a wedding, with polished shoes and a wilting flower in the button hole. The hands are lightly clasped on a black book which balances upon the small mound of his stomach. The high mattress of the bed creates a catafalque for the body, raising it up high. Even in this sallow light the pallor of the face is a bloodless blue.

Taliesin is no different from other boys of his age, he has seen scores of dead people: men with arrows in their backs and holes in their heads, mutilated disaster victims being put into bags, women being murdered in showers. The television has displayed a rich assortment of dead. Like other boys he has simulated death in Best Man's Fall, killed Indians and shot Cowboys. He has read about death, imagined death and feigned death. But real Death has always been something that happens to people he doesn't know. He's not seen a real dead body, until now.

The boys can see that the body is a dead one and they keep a respectful distance. The bed is fully made, the hands are unnaturally still, there is no slow rise of the chest. They know that it is dead and yet still they wait, half expecting the body to move and say something to them and make fools of their eyes. For some time an instinctive reverence keeps them from taking a closer look. The body is somehow more eloquent and wise than any living thing; it humbles them to the soles of their feet. When Luc speaks his voice is shockingly vibrant.

'What's that smell?' he asks.

There is a sweet perfume; a low and dull odour which is neither repulsive nor attractive. It smells like something on the turn, it's a very living smell. This smell is probably what they call the smell of death, Taliesin thinks. He sees the hands. He walks towards the body now, breaking its spell. There will be no need to put a mirror over the mouth to see if the faintest breath can steam it up, and there won't be a pulse in the blue hand. The smell and the dead calm are all the postmortem needed. But there is one last rite to perform. He takes the hand, recoiling slightly from its otherness – it isn't living at all; it has no warmth and no purpose. It is shocking to remember that this hand once enhanced life. He holds the cold thing there and pinches the skin on the back of the hand. The Skin Clock stays pinched, all its elasticity gone. It is late in the life. It has stopped.

'What are you doing?' Hoop asks.

'I think he is dead,' Taliesin says.

Billy's hands are resting on the poise-improving Holy Bible that he used for balancing on Taliesin's head. Taliesin lifts the other cold hand and opens the book. A smell of leather mingles with the smell of death. He reads the first line, which every Believer had to know by heart. The wording is different – this is a very old edition – but the gist is the same. Taliesin closes the book and replaces it beneath the hands.

He can't quite connect this body with Billy. Where is the warmth that flowed through these hands? Where is the spark that lit up the eyes? It is Billy's body but Billy is no longer in it. The essence of Billy isn't here. There are four bodies in this room but only three people.

'How did he die?' Luc asks.

'He was ill,' Taliesin says.

Taliesin pictures x-rays and sees Billy coughing. Perhaps with so much energy going out of his body he had none in reserve, no resistance against illness. But he senses that Billy's spirit is slipping away and is, even now, moving unseen and through nothing that can touch it. How far has it travelled – that spirit? Has it reached its destination yet, or can it be arrested in transit before it takes up permanent residence elsewhere? If they act quickly enough couldn't they bring it back and bring Billy back to life? The power of life is in that spirit. Lazarus slept for four days before Jesus brought him back from beyond the sweet-smelling stage. There may still be time and there is a man who should know for sure.

The Fox's hole isn't far. In his casual clothes the preacher no longer looks like a preacher. He is flustered at this unexpected call and ready to turn them away, as if they were collecting for Guy Fawkes or some fake cause. But it isn't November. Then he recognizes Taliesin.

'Ah, it's salt, isn't it.'

Taliesin is still thinking of that spirit slipping away at the speed of spirits. The expedient of saving a life helps him cut through the protocol and get to the point.

'You must come quickly. Billy Evans is dead. We just found him. I don't think he's been dead for four days.'

The preacher gives the queerest look. This is too odd to be a lie.

'What? Where is he?'

'In his bedroom, Sir.'

'Let me fetch my coat. Wait there.'

The preacher is a Grown-Up who has difficulty communicating with children. He keeps a physical and verbal distance from the three boys as they walk to the bungalow, taking long loping strides and speaking long looping words. He says that he isn't fully prepared to trust their report until he's seen the body and established the authenticity of their story.

At the house he asks them to show him the body, telling them to wait outside the bedroom. He then makes a call to the hospital and talks in sombre tones about a man being dead and needing a doctor to do a postmortem.

'You boys had better wait for the doctor. She may need to ask you some questions about what time you found him. Billy Evans is dead,' he says, in a superior tone, as if discovering this truth for the first time.

'But what about trying to resurrect him?' Taliesin persists.

Preece hums a sigh and waves a dismissive arm at this. He'd like to get rid of this salty boy. 'We can't do that. If you'd found him earlier we might have been able to resuscitate him. I'm not in the business of resurrections. I am not Jesus.'

'But Lazarus was dead for four days when Jesus found him,' Taliesin pleads. 'If we don't try it'll be too late.' He can see the spirit arriving at its final destination, unable to return. Taliesin wishes he'd tried to resurrect Billy himself, without the preacher's aid.

Preece continues to smile and patronize.

'God chose to let Lazarus live – that was his decision. He did it so that others might see his power and believe in it. He didn't go around resurrecting every Tom, Dick and Harry. Besides, Billy Evans was an old man. He's lived his three score and ten. You must accept that now.'

Doesn't the preacher know that we will never know what God can do until we ask him? Even Hooper has discovered that.

The preacher is clearly glad to hear a vehicle backing into the drive. He uses the kerfuffle of ambulance men as a convenient diversion from these difficult metaphysical questions. The boys' sense of being marginalized only increases with the arrival of the doctor – a young woman with a black bag that looks big enough to hold a soul. The doctor and the preacher talk to each other out of earshot. He then shows her into the bedroom and there is another long wait. Taliesin stares at the light under the bedroom door. Can't they see that the body is useless and that it's the spirit they need to look for? It'll be too late, he thinks, he'll be there by now.

The Grown-Ups emerge speaking in the resigned past tense of the obituary.

'Did you know him?' the doctor is asking the preacher.

'He was an occasional member of my congregation for a few years.'

'Does he have any relatives we can contact?' the doctor asks.

'Do you know, I'm not sure that he does. He wasn't married. The boy might know, though. These are the boys who found him. Taliesin, do you know if Mr Evans had any relatives?'

'He had a sister.'

'Still living?'

'I don't know.'

'I'd like to ask you some more questions later,' the doctor asks.

Collectively the boys decide that they don't like the doctor and that playing dumb is the best way of answering her. Taliesin looks down at the floor depressed at this bureaucracy. He feels Hooper's consoling hand at his shoulder. He looks and sees a hand without the full five.

In time the body is brought out shrouded in a white sheet which is pulled up over the face as if it were taboo to see it. Why is everyone whispering? Taliesin thinks. Do they think Billy might be upset at the news? Do they in some way cling to the notion that he's still able to hear them?

It is fully dark outside and the lights of the ambulance are an extra-terrestrial neon and the van might be a spaceship transporting the body away to the heavens. The radio is still on and they listen to the *Six O'Clock News*. Nothing about these events is reported.

There are more questions from the doctor who is overly cheery and matter of fact about it all. She confirms the diagnosis and establishes the cause as being heart failure brought on by lack of oxygen. Taliesin would like to correct this verdict with the suggestion that Billy sacrificed his own health by saving the health of others but he isn't asked for his opinion, he is only asked more questions. What time did you find him? What was the purpose of your visit? Why didn't you call the ambulance? The boys continue to honour the age-apartheid and say nothing. To avoid aggravation Preece intercedes for her, pointing out that Taliesin is a little upset, being a friend of Mr Evans's.

The doctor then offers condolences to them all, adding that at least Billy Evans died peacefully in his sleep. He is at rest now, she says. How can she be sure? Taliesin wonders. He was already resting when he died. Did he pass from one kind of sleep to another? Where have you gone to, Billy? You're not under the sheet in the empty shell of your body. That isn't it. You haven't suddenly just stopped. I can feel you still. Or is that just my memory setting aside a wide and expansive place of honour for you? What's happened to the force that poured through your hands – is that where I'll find you? That picture I have of you in my head now, so clear, so real, that isn't you is it? Where's the essence of you, the thing that lit you? Where have you gone to, Billy, and what will you do when you get there? Have you gone to heaven? Can anything in heaven need healing? Do angels suffer from colds and bad backs? Perhaps they inadvertently fly into each other and break their wings. What happens when you arrive? Will someone be waiting with a register, totting up the good deeds against the bad? Surely they'll let you pass through.

The doctor doesn't look as though she will have the answer to any of these questions. Her job isn't to look beyond the thing that's left behind. She examines and assesses the body only. She isn't qualified to discern the whereabouts of the spirit. The medical evidence is overwhelming and undeniable. The doctor says so and the preacher agrees. Billy is dead and that's a fact.

Taliesin feels his own life buzzing. It is there now, electric inside him. There at the back of his head – but not part of his body. Billy said that the spirit doesn't die. It doesn't die, he said . . . It doesn't. Where will I be when I am not me? He will be spirit. That's his spirit now inside him. The others have it: the doctor, the preacher, his friends, his family, they have it too but it only truly buzzes when it comes into contact with God. When it recognizes Him, it leaps and reaches out as surely and firmly as a hand picking an apple from a tree.

CHAPTER TWENTY-ONE

❧

HE TRIES TO CHEAT TIME by walking slowly to catch his bus. Of course, his slow pacing makes no impression on the ticking of the seconds and the passing of the minutes. As he reaches the halfway point of the walk, where the hill levels off and begins to descend, he looks into the sun and holds his gaze on it for as long as he can before being forced to draw away and blink. Ever since his father told him that a person could blind themselves by staring directly at the sun for longer than ten seconds, Taliesin has tried to look at it, always pulling his gaze away at the seventh or eighth second and seeing yellow black sun shadows in his head for minutes after.

His atlas tells him that we can't actually see the sun. It says we only see the light of the sun. We know the sun is there because we see the light testifying to its existence. God is like that, Taliesin thinks. He cannot know for certain what God is or looks like but he can look at the light that God gives and guess at the character and substance of the source. He can follow that light back to the place from which it radiates.

Six, seven, eight, nine . . . the brightness forces him to look away and clench his eyes closed. Yellow black suns fill his head and when he opens his eyes the suns are still obscuring his vision, blurring everything. He looks down at his feet and sees suns; at what he thinks is the path and sees suns; back at the sky and sees suns. For a second he thinks that he must have been counting too slowly; that he did in fact pass the ten second mark. He blinks some more, like someone trying to rid themselves of a splinter. Still the black orbs persist. Ahead of him suns block the path and he thinks he can see someone. He blinks rapidly to see who it is. Still only black blinking suns. He carries on walking, a little unsure of his tread.

When he arrives at the grocers he sees a man bending in front of the fruit stand and turning, with an apple in the palm of his extended hand. The figure is standing in front of the sun and Taliesin is forced to squint. He hears a voice and looking up he sees that the grocer is holding out the fruit to him and saying something.

'Hello? Well, do you want the apple, or not?'

Taliesin takes the apple and holds it firmly, pressing its hardness against his chest to see if it is an apparition.

'You're off in your own world. You've been reading one of your fantastic books again,' the grocer says.

'I looked at the sun for more than ten seconds,' Taliesin explains. 'It's strong, that light.'

'Summer isn't that far off,' the Walrus says, twiddling the ends of his curling moustache.

'My mother is getting married in the summer,' Taliesin says. 'Not in a chapel, though. It's in a kind of office. She's not going to have any guests.'

The grocer says nothing, he just looks and takes stock of the boy. Taliesin thinks he is going to say something like, 'You have grown, you know'. But if the grocer is thinking it, he keeps it to himself.

Taliesin squeezes the apple and thanks him for it. The black sun stains in his head have disappeared. Everything has a perfect clarity again; the outline, the substance and the colour, all vividly certain. There is a whole pageant of fruit in front; a curving sky above; detailed ground beneath. The grocer has pink lips, the road is a smoky grey, the apple is the right weight in his hand.